I0577696

RUSH

NIGHTHAWKS SERIES BOOK FIVE

LISA LANG BLAKENEY

WRITERGIRL PRESS

LISA LANG BLAKENEY
Love reading novels featuring hot alpha men who fall for smart women?
Then join MY VIP MAILING LIST at http://LisaLangBlakeney.com/VIP
and get a free book just for joining!

Copyright © 2021 Lisa Lang Blakeney.
All rights reserved.
Published by: Writergirl Press

FOLLOW ME
Follow me on Facebook
Join my Fan Group
Follow me on Amazon
Follow me on Bookbub
Follow me on Instagram

LICENSE NOTE

This book is a work of fiction. Any similarity to real events, people, or places is entirely coincidental. All rights reserved. This book may not be reproduced or distributed in any format without the permission of the author, except in the case of brief quotations used for review.

The author acknowledges the trademarked status of products referred to in this book and acknowledges that trademarks have been used without permission.

This book contains mature content, including graphic sex. Please do not continue reading if you are under the age of 18 or if this type of content is disturbing to you.

WHAT READERS ARE SAYING ABOUT LISA

"Lisa writes books that are intense. Explosive. Panty Melting. Raw. Exposed. Angst. Multifaceted."

"Cover to cover, page by page every word was amazing. This author is amazing and her work is even more amazing. She really can get all the details and words to sound great together."

"As soon as I picked up book 1 I was addicted to this series. I couldn't wait for this one to come out!"

"I definitely recommend this series to readers. It was the first of its kind that I have read, and I was not disappointed. 5 Stars!"

This is a book dedicated to all my readers who love a Nighthawk man.

BOOKS BY LISA

The Masterson Series

Devour this addictive series about the possessive bad boy, Roman Masterson, who falls hard and fast for the girl he's promised his family to protect.

Masterson

Masterson Unleashed

Masterson In Love

Masterson Made

Joseph Loves Juliette

Masterson Box Set

Masterson Next Generation Series

The crazy hot fruit doesn't fall far from the tree. Dive into this second generation of Masterson men!

Knox - Knox & Gigi

Bronx - Bronx & Karma

Seven - Coming soon!

The King Brothers Series

Dive into this series of interconnected standalones featuring 3 alpha hot brothers and the women they lay claim to without apology.

Claimed - Camden & Jade

Indebted - Cutter & Sloan

Broken - Stone & Tiny

Promised - All King Brothers

King Brothers Box Set

The Nighthawk Series

Sexy & sweet sports romances set in the professional world of football. All standalones.

Saint - Saint & Sabrina

Wolf - Cooper & Ursula

Diesel - Mason & Olivia

Jett - Jett & Adrienne

Rush - Rush & Mia

Freak - Freak & Willow

Brick - Brick & Kaya

Dak - Coming soon

The Club

(Also known as Bleu Whiskey)

Dark, age-gap, serialized romance set in the underbelly of Los Angeles.

Patreon (early access)

Kindle Vella

Radish

MASTERSON

Meet Alpha Roman Masterson

Free For A Limited Time!

"Our passion is incredibly intense. The connection between us borders on the possessive. Our feelings are absolutely forbidden. The question now is…what the f*ck are we going to do about it?"

DOWNLOAD NOW
Available exclusively through this link.

INTRODUCTION

A one-click, *ooh* they're cute, best friends-to-lovers romance and delicious love story with the yummiest tight end in the NFL.

From bestselling author Lisa Lang Blakeney comes a new contemporary football romance between a strong and silent tight end and the carefree woman who has always had his heart.

I unexpectedly lost my job
And am in debt up to my eyeballs
Until my best friend a.k.a. my lucky charm– Rush
Gets me my dream job working for the NFL

We're best friends so this will be fun and easy
At least that's what I thought until I actually started the job
And one of his teammates asks me out on a date
Then Rush starts acting strange

Now our friendship feels like it's totally changing

And I think we're both in over our heads
Drowning in feelings and desire that can no longer be
ignored
But clearly frightens us both

Um, you see where this is going, right?

ONE

MIA

University Of Miami

THERE's something about the golden crackle of an enormous bonfire that I'm drawn to yet also frightens me. Perhaps it's the dazzling flicker of the flames or the powerful feeling that grows inside my chest as I watch the luminous flames grow in height with each log thrown on the pyre. Something about it seems so ominous.

Maybe in a past life I was a witch who danced in the moonlight in nothing but her birthday suit, but tonight I dance with all of my teammates around the flames in joyful anticipation of our playoff game tomorrow against our rival, Florida State.

It's so much fun to let loose after two weeks of intense preparation for one of the most important volleyball games of our lives. Not only do we want to win, but there will be a scout at the game for the US Olympic team and playing in the Olympics has always been my dream.

"You're like a Wiccan minus the flowy white dress spinning around the fire like that."

I spread my arms even wider as I twirl around the bonfire in my bare feet, laughing boisterously at my teammate, Pearl.

"You know I love to dance. This is the best stress reliever before a big game."

I grow dizzy and almost fall to the moist Miami sand beneath my feet when my best friend, Rush, catches me just in the knick of time.

"Gotcha."

I grin goofily when I see his stern face looking down at me while many of the other girls around the fire swoon. Rush is a big deal at our university. He plays tight end for the Hurricanes and is one of the more popular players to fantasize about.

"All those nights at the gym are paying off," I say impressed. "You caught me with one arm and it's not even shaking."

Pearl plops herself into the sand and gawks at my unassuming friend like most girls do here at school whenever Rush is around.

"You're going to break your neck one day," he fusses. "Where are your sneakers?"

"Ha, you sound like my *paw-paw*."

"You need to be careful. You could step on a cracked seashell or a freakin' beer bottle and put a hole in your foot. Then there'll be no playoff game in your future."

I ignore my curmudgeon of a friend. He's a worrier by nature and isn't the best with social graces and niceties, but I know he means well.

"Isn't the fire magnificent?" I ask him.

"Yes, yes, the fire is big," he answers dismissively.

"I can totally feel my ancestors sending me bountiful vibes tonight, Rush. We're going to kill it tomorrow. We're going to crush Florida State!" I say loud enough for everyone to hear.

"Yeah!!" My teammates collectively holler back. "Woo-hoo!"

"Of course you're going to win," Rush affirms. "You're the best team in the region."

"You're going to be at the game, right?"

"I have my own game to get ready for. I have to practice."

"Rush Bacchetti! I can't believe you."

"What do you want me to do, Mia? You know coach doesn't make exceptions about practice, even when it comes to you. He'll bench me if I don't show up."

I met Rush my freshman year. While we were both recruited to the university on athletic scholarships, let's just say he has always been a lot more precious to the college than I ever was. Football players are like gods to this place and are treated as such. It only took me a second to understand the athletic hierarchy once I stepped inside the football team's athletic dorm. It was like a damn Four Seasons Hotel compared to our accommodations, which looked more like a tidy Motel 6.

I was invited over by another ballplayer, an older sophomore, who probably wanted to get inside my pants that day, but once I started raising hell about the differences in the dorms and the privilege I was seeing (like free vending machines for them while ours were coin-operated), he was completely turned off. He shook his head and walked away, wanting no parts of my equality for all hissy fit.

Rush, on the other hand, was interested.

"What's wrong with your dorm?" he asked, genuinely curious.

"Do you want to see the hovel they've got the volleyball queens of this university staying in?"

"Sure, I'm down."

From that moment forward, the two of us became friends and kindred spirits. We would grab lunch often and go to each other's games for support. We'd often sit on campus and talk about our favorite classes or our least favorite professors. We were an unlikely pair; sort of like The Odd Couple. He was quiet and focused, and I was bubbly and all over the place. He came from a solid two parent family and I was from an emotionally unavailable single mom. He seemed to ace his classes with little effort, and I had to study throughout the night just to pass a chapter quiz. He held people at a distance and I always gave people too much credit, but something about our friendship works.

People have never understood it, but I'm smart enough to know that you don't meet many people like Rush in a lifetime which is why I have always valued our friendship and definitely depend on it. And while I'd never say this out loud, because I know it would make him feel guilty, it makes me nervous that Rush won't be at one of the most important games of my career.

He's my good luck charm.

When Rush comes to our games, I know there will be lots of loud claps and cheers for us because when anyone from the football team attends our matches; the groupies are sure to follow. That means we'll have a large crowd of spectators, which is always fuel for an athlete's motivation. More importantly though, Rush is my biggest fan. If he's not going to be there tomorrow, it will feel like an essential part of the team will be missing.

I grab a bottle of 100% cranberry juice out of the cooler of beer and hand it to him.

"You thirsty?"

"Wow, I thought, there'd only be beer here. You volleyball chicks are drunks."

"You know I wouldn't forget that you're the most *disciplined* football player in the entire university, so I bought you some juice."

He knows that using disciplined is my code word for describing how regrettably predictable he is. Throughout our years here on campus, he's been known to be the fun police. He's pulled me away from more frat parties than I care to remember and away from school clubs that in his words "were nothing but a distraction".

"Only the disciplined players get into the pros, Bird."

"I know, I know, but you only live once and if I want to drink a beer before the game, I'm going to have one. It ain't going to kill me," I retort. "I'm sure plenty of Olympians drink a beer or two."

"Why do you call her Bird?" Pearl asks Rush with the goofiest grin across her face. I forgot she was even there for a moment.

"She sings all the damn time," he tells her.

"Just like a bird," I say, imitating one by flapping my arms as if they were wings.

One of my other teammates changes the song on the portable bluetooth speaker and it's a Black Eyed Peas classic. I can't help myself and start dancing around the bonfire like a possessed woman.

"You can't possibly be drunk yet," Pearl comments, laughing at my dance.

"She's not," Rush tells her. "That's her totally sober."

"I drink beer because I genuinely enjoy the taste and

not because of any way it may alter my state. A girl like me is drunk on life."

Everything I said was true. Regardless of my crappy home life, I'm just a genuinely cheerful person. I was born that way.

I stop in front of Rush and try mimicking a dance I saw a little boy doing in a viral video. I do it because he thought the video was just as hysterical as I did.

"Seriously?" He cracks a smile and slides his hand through his thick mane of chestnut-colored hair. "You look like a zombie in a hip hop dance class."

"This song reminds me of the sixth grade," I say as I continue to exuberantly dance. "My Grandmom bought me the album and didn't pay attention to the parental warnings. She just assumed they were a squeaky clean group."

"Rookie Grandmom mistake."

"Yep, it was awesome!"

I pump my fists to the rhythmic beat of *Boom Boom Pow* as Rush sinks down to the Florida sand and watches me in complete wonder.

"You're going to be completely wiped for the game if you keep this up."

"Never!" I say, panting. "Remember, Bacchetti, I won our last two mile race."

"I gave you a head start."

"Not by much!"

My favorite part of the song comes on and I start pop locking my joints like I'm in a 1980s hip-hop video.

"Damn, you're like the energizer bunny," Pearl comments.

"Did your parents tell you about MTV when they were young?" I ask them, slightly out of breath. "It was like the only place they could see their favorite artists perform when they were kids. Isn't that nuts?"

"My parents didn't watch cable," Pearl says.

"Rush?" He doesn't answer at first. "Isn't that wild?"

"Yeah, yeah," he finally replies, totally ignoring me now and paying more attention to the texts coming in on his phone.

"Who's that?" I ask him.

"Kayla."

"Ooh, that's the pretty girl from California in the school of business, right?"

"Yeah."

"She sending you dirty texts?"

"Nah, Bird, she's not like that."

"I bet." I give him the side eye.

All girls are like *that* when it comes to Rush. I once saw a girl wait forty-five minutes to say hello and hand him a greeting card on Valentine's Day. It was the cutest yet saddest thing I've ever seen. Rush prefers words over cards. He thinks greeting cards are a waste of money.

After the song ends, I plop down next to him totally exhausted yet oddly invigorated.

"Whew!"

"Gross, you're sweating."

He pushes my head off of his shoulder.

"It's the heat of my ancestors calling to me."

"It's because you were jumping around like your pants were on fire."

"It's called dancing."

"If that's what you want to call that. You've got like fifteen more minutes and then we need to leave. I've got curfew and so do you last time I checked."

"Alright, *paw-paw*." Then I stand again. "But just one more dance."

***

On game day, I complete all of my usual rituals. I brush my teeth for exactly four minutes. I wear my lucky pair of sunshine yellow panties. I lay naked on my bed for exactly ten minutes and meditate with four crystals in the center of my chest. And finally, I make my pre-game phone call between me and Rush.

The call is even more important today because I know I won't get to see his scowling face in the stands. When he calls, he only has to say a few words. I know what they mean. We've been saying them to each other since we met freshman year.

"World domination greetings, Mia."

"World domination greetings, Rush."

"Talk to you after you beat their asses?"

"Affirmative."

Then we hang up, and all is right with the world.

This game is going to be epic.

***

Your life can change in moments... even seconds, and no one ever told me. I probably wouldn't have believed them if they had.

Our game against our conference rival is going fantastically as we knew it would. Our team is stronger and faster and we have insane chemistry, but as I leap high to spike the ball like I have a million times before, my left ankle buckles when I land.

Then my left knee pops.

And then the most intense pain radiates throughout my body.

And I cry out for God.

I already know what I've done. I'm in my senior year of physical therapy school. I've completely torn my ACL. No doctor has to tell me. I can feel it. It's the injury every athlete most fears.

The small crowd of spectators grows quiet as I lay in the sand writhing in pain and watching my entire future disintegrate before my eyes. The smoke and ashes of a promising Olympic career, up in flames just like the beautiful bonfire I attended last night.

I'll have to go back home to Philly.

To a mother who won't be happy to have another mouth to feed in her home.

Even worse, I'll be going back to a life of musicless, colorless, cold mediocrity.

And for me, that's no life at all.

TWO

MIA

Four Years Later
Northern New Jersey

I'm singing Adele's classic *Rolling In The Deep* completely off key, with the window down, arm hanging out of my sea green Prius like I don't have a care in the world, because when you're singing that woman's songs, you must sing them with a full heart and a clear mind or you won't feel the words where you're meant to feel them — in your gut.

When I stop at the red light, there's a woman and a small boy who turn their heads upon hearing my powerful vocals and giggle. That's fine. I've never pretended that I was anybody's Aretha Franklin, but that doesn't mean you're ever going to stop me from singing loud and proud. I get it honestly. My Grandma was a second soprano in the church choir and couldn't sing a lick either. You could hear her from twenty pews back, but nobody gave a damn, particularly her.

When I pull into my job's parking lot, my mood

completely shifts. I turn Adele off and start feeling around the passenger seat for my cell phone. Somebody in that building has to call a tow truck right now. A visitor without handicapped plates, stickers or tags is parked in my spot and I'll be damned if I'm going to limp my ass all the way from the back of the parking lot to the front entrance.

"Mr. B?"

"That you, Mia?"

"Yes, sir."

"What can I do you for?"

"There's some random car parked in the main handicapped space near the east entrance. No tags or anything."

I know it's not technically *my* spot, but visitors wouldn't be parking in the East parking lot. This lot is for students and staff only, and I know for a fact that no one in my building has a physical limitation besides me.

"It's probably some clueless summer student."

"There are no other available spaces, Mr. B."

"I can call the tow man, Miss Mia, but they're going to take an awfully long time to get here."

Ugh.

"How about you just swing around the back of the building, part next to my truck, and I'll take you on up in the freight elevator," Mr. B generously offers.

"I knew you'd have a solution. Perfect, here I come."

Mr. Billy Hayes has probably been on the building support staff of Phoenixville University for over twenty-five years; maybe even longer than that. He knows each building on the campus like the back of his hand and is one of the sweetest men alive. I'm very lucky to work as a sports physical therapist at a university with such down-to-earth faculty and staff who care about each other.

I park my Prius, which I've named the green goblin, next to Mr. B's truck, grab my messenger bag and my cane when he walks over to my car and opens it.

Since I blew out my knee in college, I walk with a limp and sometimes need the help of a cane depending on how I feel that day. Today, I woke up with pain at a level four and so I know I'll need my walking stick, but what I don't need are people making it obvious that I need that help. Of course, Mr. B is a seventy-one-year-old grandfather of three who is old-school to his core. There's no way he isn't going to hold every door open for me he can to help me inside. I have no choice but to accept his kindness.

"Can I take your bag, Miss Mia?"

Oh, and he addresses everyone with a miss or mister before their name, no matter their age. He says that's the way people were taught to speak to each other in his generation. It's just his way.

"Thank you, Mr. B."

As much as it pains me to hand over my bag to him, I do. I know that protesting would be a moot point. Sometimes you've just got to let a gentleman be a gentleman, no matter their age. That's one gem and jewel my grandmother taught me long before she passed away from ovarian cancer. Grandma's death was swift and pointless, and I miss her so much; I don't think my mother will ever recover from her loss either.

"Did you hear the rumors, Miss Mia?"

"No, about who?" I smile.

Mr. B is always a good source for university faculty drama. Apparently, professors sleep around with each other much more than you would think.

"Not who, but what. There's supposed to be some

serious changes coming around here because of the tough economy."

This isn't fun news at all.

"Changes for who?"

I hope they aren't going to lay off Mr. B. He has a wife on dialysis and his daughter plus two of those three grandchildren live with him. The last thing he needs is his steady income taken away.

"Staff cuts. All the professors are worried something awful."

"The University claims there will be budget cuts every year, Mr. B, but something always comes through," I assure him.

"Hope you're right. We've been really lucky so far. Other institutions have seen complete programs wiped out."

"I'm sure there's some rich Silicon Valley dude who's itching to give away some money to a worthy university. We're small but mighty, Mr. B. People have heard of us. A United States House Representative attended here. The money will definitely come."

I speak the words into existence because I need to. I'm behind on almost every single one of my bills ever since I bought the green goblin. Even though I bought her used, I made the big mistake of buying a car with money I thought was coming via our annual cost-of-living raise. But the raise never happened, and neither did a bonus, and now I'm up to my eyeballs in bills.

"You're such a breath of fresh air, Miss Mia. I wish more folks were as positive thinking as you. You could give my daughter a lesson or two."

"I don't have kids yet though," I tell him. "Your daughter is dealing with a lot of other things that just aren't on my radar yet."

"True. Ain't gonna lie, my grandkids are a handful."

Both of us chuckle as we continue my slow trek to the freight elevator. Mr. B takes me to the second floor of the building and escorts me to the physical therapy office that I share with three other therapists.

"I'll call the tow guy, but you can stay parked next to my truck all day. It's no problem," he offers, after handing me my bag.

"Thanks, I appreciate it."

"Have a good day."

"And you have a great one. Remember what I said, things are going to be just fine."

MIA

I CAME to Phoenixville University during the fall after I graduated from the University of Miami with my physical therapy degree. Although PT was my major, becoming a therapist was never part of my plan.

I always thought I'd be an Olympic volleyball player and then playing in professional tournaments in other countries, maybe later becoming a coach. I never imagined that I'd be stuck in a building all day helping other promising athletes with their rehabilitation at twenty-five years old. But I don't have the luxury of being a whiner, and so I had to make an adjustment to my goals and dreams. *You do the best with the hand you've been dealt* is another Grandma Taylor gem and jewel I try my best to live my life by.

"Morning, Mia."

"Morning, Jacob."

"Can I see you in my office?"

"Sure."

I take a seat in my supervisor's tiny office and rub my knee while we talk. It's not unusual for us to go over the client schedule for the day on a Monday, which is why I brought a pad and pen with me into the office.

"Who's on deck for today?" I ask.

"Mia, this is hard for me to say."

Jacob clasps his hands and sits them on the desk in front of his chest.

My face drops.

"What's hard to say?"

"I met with the folks in the financial office last week and they crunched the numbers over a dozen times."

"What numbers?"

"For our department, our therapist-to-student ratio is low compared to our budget. It's one of the lowest in the state and we're a small university. We have four therapists on staff when in reality two therapists could serve the same amount of students if we restructured our therapeutic model."

"So you're going to move two of us somewhere else in the athletic department?"

"No, Mia. I'm sorry, but I'm going to have to let you and Addison go."

I unconsciously clench my jaw.

"You're firing me?"

Although I've been on the PT team here for four years, I realize that I still am one of the last people hired. All the other therapists have been here much longer than me, including Addison.

"Yes, I'm sorry."

"You didn't even give me a heads up, Jacob."

"I'm sorry, but the decision wasn't finalized until over the weekend. I was instructed not to say anything to you until then."

"But you had to know they were thinking about doing

this. I could have looked for another position. I have rent due. I have bills."

"All I can say is that I'm so sorry. It's tough working for a small institution like ours. Change happens overnight, and it often isn't pretty."

He stares at me massaging my knee and I can smell the pity coming off of him.

I hurry my hand away.

"How much notice are you giving me?"

His guilty little eyes drop to the desktop.

"It's effective immediately."

"What?!"

"I'm sorry."

He keeps apologizing as if the words are going to soothe the sting of what is happening in this room right now.

"This feels like I'm being fired, not laid off."

"I was able to negotiate paying you for the rest of the week. It was the best I can do. At least now you'll get paid while you look for something else."

My heart sinks.

A week's pay won't even cover the back rent.

"And my health insurance?"

I have a consultation with a new surgeon coming up and I still get regular therapies for my knee but neither of those come cheap. My insurance covers most of the bills now, but without it I won't be able to get any services. Private pay costs a fortune.

"Talk to Human Resources to verify, but I'm sure you'll get some sort of temporary coverage to tide you over until you find a more permanent solution."

This is a nightmare.

It's not going to be easy to find someone willing to hire a

physical therapist with a physical limitation of her own. It's just not done.

My college volleyball coach, Dr. Lynn, was able to pull some strings and get me a full ride into the Master's residency program with Phoenixville after putting in a good word for me after graduation. The deal was I would enroll in their newly accredited master's PT program and simultaneously work as a resident my first year of school and then become a full-time employee while I studied to pass my certification exam. It was a great opportunity for me, and I've been here ever since.

Luckily, it was a hop, skip and a jump away from Rush. He was drafted to the Nighthawks straight out of Miami and owns a mansion in a wealthy Jersey township about thirty minutes from me. I don't think he bought something in New Jersey because I live and work here, though. Most New York ballers live in Northern New Jersey because of the better cost of living and cushy suburban lifestyle. We were both just fortunate to have fates that merged in the same location.

"I just bought my car," I say, thinking out loud.

"If I hear of another position, you'll be the first person I call," he says solemnly. "And I'll be sure to write you a great recommendation letter."

"Sure, Jacob."

The tips of his ears turn a blush red.

"I know it isn't much, but it's the best I can do, Mia."

My guess is that Jacob is genuinely upset that he's been the one tasked to letting me go, but it doesn't make me feel much better about things. I've built a life on the security I thought this job afforded me.

To some people I probably make a lot of money, but it's all relative because I spend more than I make. Case in point: I moved into a higher rent apartment to be closer to the university (which I'm behind on), I purchased the green goblin a few months ago because everyone in Jersey needs a car and it was energy efficient, and beyond my regular bills I send money home to my mother every month.

My mom is a textbook case of a woman who had a child too young and resents the baby she had with the absentee father. After he bailed, she never wanted me. At most, she tolerated me. The only genuine love I ever felt was from my grandmother, and now that she's gone, I'm basically a paycheck to my mom.

My mom's name is Amanda, but people (including me) call her Mandy for short. She's an underemployed server who lives in my grandmother's house, which she has to pay the real estate taxes on or she'll lose it. She's late on the taxes every year, like clockwork. In her world, I make a fortune and should pay the taxes for her, but in truth I'm robbing Peter to pay Paul. I'm barely eking out a living at all, but I'll be damned if I'm going to let my Grandmom's house go into foreclosure. Her home meant the world to her. So I send home money to help. Now I don't know how the hell I'm going to manage to do all of it.

I limp out of Jacob's office and into the empty main therapy room. I have two calls to make as I clean out my locker and clear the hard drive of my work computer. First, I've got to get Billy to come back up here and take me back to my car. And second, I need my best friend to tell me everything's going to be okay.

I need to talk to Rush.

FOUR

TRAINING CAMP
Central New Jersey

I WAS DRAFTED as a second-round pick to The New York Nighthawks right out of college, and I've seen a lot of drama in these last three years, but training camp is the most intense that it's ever been. There are two players who absolutely despise each other and that makes for a great deal of tension on and off the field. It's not an ideal situation, especially when one of those players is a star running back who the team paid a lot of money for.

We've just had our early morning drills, and it's time for a mid-morning break. I peel my jersey off and am removing some of my protective gear when I turn around to see what the commotion is.

It's them.

It started on social media, continued in practice, and now it's still bubbling over into the locker room. Proctor and Samuels are at it again.

"What's up?" Proctor (the running back) throws his hands up and starts moving aggressively toward Samuels (an offensive lineman). "You're supposed to be one of Alabama's finest, and you can't even see when the biggest man on the field is coming for your quarterback?"

They're arguing about a practice session earlier.

"It was your job to run the ball," Samuels says in defense of himself. "Just worry about that and stop fumbling the damn thing."

"Just admit that you don't know what the fuck you're doing out there."

I drop some of my pads on the locker room floor with a thud. I don't want to hear all of this bickering. They're like two little annoying gnats. I just want to swat them away. We've got the rest of the day to spend with each other and God knows it can't go on like this.

"Just admit that this doesn't have shit to do with how I'm playing," Samuels challenges.

"Oh, so you want to take it there?"

"Let's take it all the fuck the way there."

"What you did was foul," Proctor spits his words angrily.

"And what you said about me on Twitter was fucked up. My family reads that shit."

Distinctive low muttering spreads throughout the locker room. I stay off of social media so I don't know what they're talking about, but I know it ain't good. I've never seen two players more at odds than these two are with each other. Whatever it is, it isn't about football, this is personal.

"She's my mother, you asshole!" Proctor exclaims.

"Dayummmm!" the entire room explodes.

"Ain't nobody fucking your dusty ass mama," Samuels retorts dismissively.

"Dayummmm!" the room exclaims again.

"What did you just say?"

"You heard me."

This is going south really fast. If there's one thing I learned after being in countless locker rooms is that no man can stomach when you talk about their mother, especially in this situation. Evidently Proctor thinks Samuels slept with his mom and that shit is never going to fly. You don't sleep with any of your teammate's women, especially the women who gave birth to them. That's like fucking with Saint Theresa.

"Fuck you, man!"

Proctor swings on Samuels and basically sucker punches him. Samuels reactively holds his jaw for a moment, but then quickly reacts. He tosses his heaviest pads to the ground and then the two of them go blow for blow. Samuels may have mistakingly hit one of the defensive backs during the scuffle because the next thing I know most of the team is in a full-blown brawl.

An entire locker room of grown men fighting because Samuels may or may not have boinked Proctor's mom (who for the record is a hot ass MILF) doesn't make any sense at all to me, so the only way I can explain it is that there is too much testosterone floating through their veins after a rigorous practice this morning.

I am the biggest man on the offense, maybe even the team, as far as height goes. I don't want to get involved in this shit show, but I can't allow this to fly. This isn't how a room full of grown men should be behaving.

I step in the middle of the melee to try and get some control, but get punched in the jaw by a new player named Carter for all of my efforts. Once the coaching staff hears the skirmish, they come charging back into the room.

"What the hell?"

Many of our coaches and trainers were pro players themselves and are big and fit, so they have no problem forcing themselves in the middle of us to break up the fight.

"Break it up, idiots. Is this pee-wee ball? Get your asses out of my locker room if you can't act like professionals!" Coach angrily demands.

After things settle down, Carter approaches me to apologize. His right fist is tucked securely under his left armpit.

"I didn't even see it was you when I swung, man. I'm so sorry."

"Right."

"Yo, man, your jaw must be made out of Valyrian fucking steel." He grins sheepishly. "I think I may have just broken my hand."

I shrug my shoulders because I don't give a rat's ass that Carter is hurt. He shouldn't have been fighting in the first place. None of them should have. We put our bodies on the line for a living, not for a Twitter war.

"You cut my face," I tell him, annoyed as hell as I look at myself in one of the locker mirrors.

A player named Dixon interrupts us.

"Hey, Rush, your cell keeps ringing. I think it may be important."

"Who is it?"

Dixon is nosy. I already know he's looked at the screen.

"Someone named Bird."

I hurry to my phone and see that Mia has called me three times, back-to-back. At this time of day, my first assumption is that something must be wrong. She rarely calls me until well after practice hours and never repeatedly.

I press redial, hoping that it's nothing I'll have to kill someone over, because while I won't exchange blows over childlike behavior like half of the team just did, Mia is somebody I will wage a bloody war for.

FIVE

RUSH

"Bird?"

"Rush."

"What's wrong?" I ask on pins and needles.

"I... I was fired from my job today."

"You were what?"

"Fired. Canned. Kicked to the curb. What am I going to do, Rush?"

I hear soft cries and my heart breaks just a little.

I have heard my best friend fall apart only three times since we've met: once, when a clueless little shit dumped her our junior year of college; second, in the hospital the day she tore her ACL; and finally today.

Mia is not a crier. In fact, she's usually the most vibrant person in the room and doesn't let the heavy weight of this shitty world get to her. That's probably one of the most impressive things about her. I wish I had even a smidgeon of her indomitable spirit. I was only blessed with a talent for football.

"I take it you didn't see this coming?"

I grab a seat on one of the locker room benches as the

rest of the team cleans up the mess from the scuffle and recounts who hit who first.

"No, I mean I knew the school was tightening their belts when I didn't get a raise, and I heard some chatter about budget cuts and all of that, but I didn't think they'd fire me. I've been there almost five years. I thought I was doing a good job. I thought my job was safe."

"So it's a budgetary thing?"

"That's what they said, but you should have been there, Rush. Jacob didn't even give me any notice. I was told I was being let go one minute and then basically escorted out the door the next."

"They manhandled you?!"

I will fly so fast over to that rinky-dink college and kick somebody's ass.

"No, not literally, but it sure felt like it. I've never felt so… devalued."

More soft tears.

"It's going to be okay, Bird. You'll find something else. Something better."

The chatter in the locker room grows louder. After the argument, my teammates are still pretty excitable and still yapping about Samuels's and Proctor's drama as if they're a bunch of gossipy school girls.

"I shouldn't have called you with all this," Mia says, obviously hearing all the blathering going on around me. "You're busy at work."

"I'm not sure what I'm doing right now should be classified as work."

"No, you're a busy man. I just needed to hear your voice for a moment, but I'm fine. I'm going to go home and get under the covers. You go back to practice. You've got a season to get ready for."

It physically pains me to hear so down. I'm not used to it. I never want to get used to it.

"How about we go out when I'm done here?"

"Out?"

"For drinks or something."

"You don't drink." She sniffles.

"That's never stopped us before. I'll pick you up at six."

Mia hesitates before she agrees.

"I can take the train and meet you in the city somewhere. I don't want to drive and have to try and find parking."

I'm from a small town in Virginia and Mia is from a big city in Pennsylvania. She is used to traveling a lot on her own on public transportation, but we did little of that where I'm from. Everyone had to drive or walk. So I'm not comfortable with her getting on a bus or train or even a damn Uber to meet me in Manhattan, especially when the sun is setting.

"It's easier for me to just pick you up."

Thankfully, she doesn't give me a hard time about it. Usually she does.

"Thanks, Rush."

"We never have to say thank you to each other, Bird."

"Right, I forgot." I can hear a hitch in her voice. She's trying not to cry again.

After we hang up, I'm pissed. Not only have I just been in the middle of a fight between teammates that resulted in a scar on my jaw, but now Mia's just been tossed on her ass by some half-ass university that she's given years of great service to. She deserved better. I always thought her immediate supervisor was incompetent. Now that's just been confirmed.

Proctor comes over to me with his tail between his legs.

Because we're using a backup quarterback this season, they look at me as the approachable leader of the offense. I'm not sure why. I barely say two words to most of them on any given Sunday.

"Rush, man, I'm sorry for today. I overreacted and things got out of hand."

"Yeah, they did."

"In my defense, he's sleeping with my mom. My MOTHER. That shit can't stand."

It's true that Proctor's mom is probably one of the youngest NFL moms I've ever seen. Her tits are high and her ass is firm and she must have given birth to his ass when she was barely a teenager. That's no excuse, though. Samuels should have never touched her, but I can see how the shit could happen.

"You can't let that personal stuff interfere with what we're doing, though. We're trying to win rings in this locker room and that's all we're fighting for or about... championship rings."

"Yeah, man, I got you."

After Proctor walks away, I contemplate whether I'm going to make the call I need to make. It's the obvious choice, a simple choice, but not the nicest thing to do.

Miranda Green works in the Human Resources division of the Nighthawks and is someone I used to sleep with on an occasional weekend off. She's an attractive woman who will make some guy a very nice wife, but our *thing* was a mistake for that very reason. She's looking for a long-term commitment and I'm not, at least not with her.

When I ended it, she was brave about it and didn't show any signs that her feelings were hurt, but I knew they were and I felt like a jerk for doing that. So now that I need to ask her for a favor, I'm wavering. It's some dickhead shit to ask a favor from someone you've hurt. She may possibly read more into it, or she just might spit in my face. I really shouldn't do this. My parents didn't raise me to be this kind of man, but the problem is that this is about Mia.

My Bird.

Between paying her bills, sending money to Mandy, and dealing with everything thing she's been through since she blew out her knee, she needs a reason to get up in the morning. She needs to work. Meaningful work.

And for Mia, I'll do just about anything.

Even if it's against my better judgement.

SIX

MIA

"Excuse me, but aren't you Rush Bacchetti?"

Rush shifts in his seat uncomfortably because he's never gotten used to being recognized out in public. It's actually one of his most endearing qualities, but the attention and his modesty about it can also be annoying. I just wish he'd just say *yes* and sign the damn cocktail napkin so his fan can be on her way. Then we can talk about more important things... like my life and that cut on his face.

"Yes, he's Rush Bacchetti," I tell her, because it's taking him entirely too long to answer.

"Really? Would you mind signing an autograph? I'm a huge fan. My entire family is."

The early 2000s Nighthawk paraphernalia she's wearing, and the defined lines across her forehead give away that the woman is probably a middle-aged, long-time fan. I don't have any problems with those women. They're true blue and deserve an autograph.

I nudge him under the table with my foot.

"Sure," Rush agrees reservedly.

He signs the napkin with a signature that looks like chicken scratch and hands it to the woman.

"Thank you."

But I knew it was too good to be true because after her come the cluckers.

Cluckers are women who aren't real football fans but groupies who strut and spread their feathers for Rush to notice so they can fuck him senseless and spend all his money. He had them in college a lot, but these adult ones are a different breed. I've seen nothing like it. They have no shame.

"I look forward to seeing you kill it this season, Rush," one of them clucks.

She's short with long dirty blonde hair and curves that are practically bursting out of her clothes at the seams. I dare her to eat one more French fry. She'll probably rip her clothes to shreds right in the middle of this bar.

Rush gives her the smallest of grins in return and thanks her.

"Thanks."

"Are you busy after this?" she asks with zero bashfulness. "Want to come to my place?"

"I'm busy all night." He responds as tactfully as he can.

"Is this your sister?" She references me as if I'm something unimportant that's in her way.

"Do we look related to you?" I retort with an obvious attitude.

Rush and I couldn't look any more different if we tried. He looks like a tall, dark, viking warrior complete with intricate tattoo sleeves and I look like a less glamorous, leggy version of the actress Zendaya but with a bigger butt. The only thing similar about us is that we're both taller than this clucker.

"I guess not," the woman scoffs. "Just thought I'd ask. You never know."

"You want a selfie or something?" Rush hurries her. "Because I'm trying to have a drink with my friend here."

"I'd love a picture!" She gushes excitedly.

She snuggles close into Rush's enormous body and holds her phone high up in the air to catch the selfie. She taps and holds the button so she can capture a series of shots.

"Thank you so much and have a good evening with your... friend here."

I plaster on the fakest of smiles.

"Nighty-night," I sing-song.

Rush punts my good leg under the table.

"Really!" I bark back. "You know I have a bum knee."

"I kicked the good leg, and I didn't even do it that hard. I toe tapped you."

"You're a professional football player. Everything you do is hard."

I'm exaggerating, of course. Rush would never hurt me, even by accident.

"I wasn't close enough to pinch your ass so a boot in the shin is the next best thing."

"It's a good thing you didn't pinch me. The last time you did that, you left a mark on my butt that my ex swore was something sexual."

"Your dudes are always so insecure." Rush lets out a low laugh. "That last one was a real dummy."

"You don't like anyone I date."

"Uh, I think that's the pot calling the kettle black."

"Ha, ha." I fake laugh. "None of the women you date can be taken seriously, so of course I don't like them."

I mimic them.

"Oh, Rush, your arms are so big. Oh, Rush, you're so amazing on the field. Oh, Rush, let's fuck each other right in the middle of this bar."

I stick a finger in my mouth to mimic the act of me vomiting. It just makes him laugh even more, which is basically the point of why I do it. Rush doesn't laugh much in public, so when he gives himself permission to let his guard down and I'm the one responsible for it, I relish those moments even more.

"Nobody talks like that, Mia. You sound like a ten-year-old child."

"Exactly my point. That's how they all sound. Their voices get all pitchy and breathy and ridiculous sounding, and I'm sure it gets a lot more pornographic when I'm not around."

"Bird, you've got to stop treating the fans like this. It's so out of character for you to be so... distrustful."

"That's what we're calling them now? Fans?"

Someone in management notices that the most popular tight end in the game is here and sends a server over to offer us a complimentary bottle for the table. It's just one perk of rolling with my bestie. I select a bottle of vodka and Rush orders a carafe of cranberry juice.

"You were supposed to order a bottle of wine. You're never going to finish an entire bottle of vodka and it's not like we can take it with us." He shakes his head. "Just mix the cranberry juice with it."

"I don't have to go to work tomorrow or ever again." I throw my hands up. "So why shouldn't I drink the damn whole thing?"

"Just don't."

There's a small stage in the bar and grill, and unbeknownst to me it's karaoke night. That's an activity which is right up my alley. They ask for volunteers as I drink my vodka and cranberry and unpack everything that's happened to me today with the one person who listens to all of my news whether it's good, bad or indifferent.

I don't even know why he puts up with me.

I'm even annoying my own self tonight.

SEVEN

MIA

"So they let me come in on a Monday morning, park in east bubblefuck, only to come inside and get fired ten minutes later. I mean, who does that?"

"Laid off," he corrects me.

"I felt like I was fired. No prior notice? Only a week's pay? Is that even legal?"

"Everybody's cutting back these days, Bird, and yes, I think it's legal."

"That doesn't make it any better. You just bought your mom and dad their dream house by the shore. Meanwhile, I don't even know if I'm going to be able to pay my rent or car note next month."

Oops, I shouldn't let that slip.

"I can lend you the money."

And this is why.

"You know I won't accept that. A Taylor woman gets herself out of her own mess."

"It's a loan, Wonder Woman. Pay it back when you figure your finances out."

"No."

"That's stupid, Mia." His face hardens. "Just take the money."

"Are you calling me stupid?" I challenge.

"Yes."

As the sun sets outside, the ambient lighting in the tavern grows brighter and Rush's cut appears more noticeable to me, or maybe I'm just drunk.

"Who put that cut on your face?"

"Work put this cut on my face."

"You let somebody beat you up at practice?" I giggle.

"Nobody beat my ass, Mia. It's football."

Rush has been playing pro football for over four years and I can't remember the last time I've seen a scar on his face. He's too fast, too big, and nobody can touch him. The one time he got into a real scuffle with someone in college, he almost got expelled because he accidentally broke the guy's wrist. Luckily he was able to plea self-defense, and the school could keep it out of the local press.

Something about his story tonight sounds off to me, but I let it go. He's a private person and I've known for a long time that I have to allow him to have his space. We don't have to share everything. It's not like he knows the extent of my financial situation. I would never burden him with that.

"Put a band-aid or something on it later. You look scarier than normal."

"I'm fine with scary."

Another woman seated adjacent to us on a bar stool has been staring at Rush during our entire conversation. I can't blame her. He is looking especially formidable tonight. His training regimen this summer has only intensified and his body has clearly benefited from it. I don't think I've ever seen a man with less body fat and more definition in my life.

I'm not sure why the woman's glares are bothering me tonight. It's nothing new. Women have always been attracted to Rush. Maybe I'm just being needy because of the terrible day I've had and I want all of his attention, or like I said before, maybe it's the vodka.

"That woman is staring at you."

"I didn't notice."

"If her eyes were laser beams, you'd be disintegrated into smithereens by now."

"What?" He laughs in only the way that Rush does. A little bit of Barney Rubble with a dash of Yosemite Sam. "You say the weirdest shit sometimes."

"You know this, man!" I say in my infamous sing-song voice.

"But seriously, Bird, let me give you a bridge loan."

A text comes into his cell phone he pays special attention to. I'm always curious as to who he has text conversations with because I fancy myself as his only friend, but of course I know that can't be true. He probably just lets me feel like it is.

"No way," I tell him again. "I'll ask my dad for money before I take some from you."

"You'll ask your deadbeat father who doesn't even call you on Christmas for money before me?"

"Yes, just because you're rich doesn't mean I should take your money. We're friends and I want to keep it that way. Money has a way of getting in between friendships and I would literally die without yours."

He stares quietly at me for a moment, and I'm not sure what he's thinking. Maybe in his eyes, I've uncomfortably overstated how I feel about him just now, but it's the truth.

"I'm not rich, Bird. There are players on my team that

make three times what I do, and I would let nothing get in between our... friendship."

I smile.

"Well, I don't know how they're living back in your hometown, but where I'm from you're rich as donkey balls."

He sends a quick text back to whoever's been blowing up his phone and returns my smile with a grin of his own.

"I've got something to tell you."

"Does it have something to do with that text you're grinning at?"

"Maybe."

"Well, spill it."

"Mmm, I'm not just going to spill it."

"So why bring it up?" I pout.

"You're going to have to pay me for this information."

"With what, dodo for brains? I've just been canned."

"With a song. It's karaoke night."

This is not really a legitimate bet. This is him trying to cheer me up. I love him, but Rush couldn't pull off a caper to save his life. He's totally transparent. But I love to sing and he's going to tell me whatever it is eventually anyway, so I gladly accept.

"Bet! What do you want to hear?"

He pauses for a moment.

"You're okay to get up there, right?" Referring to my knee.

"When am I never all right? I've got this. What do you want to hear, *paw-paw*?"

A devious grin spreads across his handsome face.

"The Bee Gees."

"You must be kidding me. You know I don't do commercial disco. Bleh!"

"I just saw this killer documentary on them and I want to hear a Bee Gees song. Take it or leave it."

"If you want disco, I'll do vintage Diana Ross or something."

"No, I want to hear the Bee fucking Gees. Take it or leave it, Bird."

"This better be juicy information you're giving me. Singing this might just damage my soul."

"It's juicy."

"Fine."

The stage is empty, so I ask the deejay if he has anything by The Bee Gees on the playlist. He does, of course, so I pick the only song I can actually stomach, *How Deep Is Your Love*. After a few notes, my muscle memory kicks in and I remember most of the words and the flow of the ballad from years of listening to my Grandmom's music collection.

I keep my eyes closed for most of the song, but when I pop them back open, Rush is staring at me with the oddest blank look as I finish belting the classic out.

I'm not sure if he pities me or is in awe of my improving singing skills.

It's always hard to tell with him.

EIGHT

RUSH

Mɪᴀ ᴍɪɢʜᴛ ʙᴇ one of the bravest women I know. The woman is practically tone deaf but has patrons in the grill entranced, especially the oddball at the table directly in front of center stage. From this view, I can see him practically foaming at the mouth as he watches her sing with her eyes closed and her long braided ponytail swaying back and forth.

She alternates singing between hushed notes and then belting out the chorus. By the third time the chorus comes around, the entire bar is singing with her and I'm quietly tapping my heel to the melody.

It's probably one of the corniest love ballads of all time and Mia is no Olivia Newton John, but there's a measure of truth you can feel from the notes when she sings them. You know she means every single word.

As she takes a theatrical bow in front of her new adoring fans, the man in front eagerly claps for her the loudest and a realization hits me like a thunderbolt. I suppose I've always known but ignored it because it had nothing to do with the relationship between us. Men don't just stare at Mia because she's a force of nature. They stare at her because they desire her. And for a split second I second guess everything I'm about to tell her tonight.

It would be like putting a drop of water into a hot frying pan.

"That was so much fun!" She plops back down in her seat.

"You were supposed to hate every minute of it," I lie, knowing full well that Mia could never hate singing in front of a crowd regardless of the song. She's too much of a performer.

"That wasn't as bad as I thought it was going to be."

"You looked like you were having fun."

"Did you like it? Did I hit all the notes? I can't believe I'm admitting this, but that song was pretty good. I guess it was one of their better ones."

"The Bee Gees are legendary. All their songs are excellent. Put some respect on their name."

She emits a genuine laugh for the first time tonight, and that's when I know I should go ahead and share my news. If it will put more smiles on her face, then it's worth the chance I'm taking.

"So... I had a brief conversation with one of the Human Resources directors for the Nighthawks, and she confirmed that there's an open position available in the therapy department."

"You must be kidding."

"My guy, Beacher, is retiring."

"The therapist you love?"

"Yeah, turns out that he's got some personal things going on and needs to take an early retirement."

"Oh my God, Rush. This is so much better than player gossip."

"Don't count all your chickens just yet. You have to interview just like everyone else, and there are a couple of rounds of interviews from what I heard. This is not a done deal just because you're my friend."

"Of course!" she says, totally blowing off my words of caution. "But I'm a believer of visualization, and I already see us riding to work together in the green goblin. It's going to be awesome!"

"I can't even fit in your car, Mia, so get that visual out of your head right now. And we won't have the same schedule anyway, so we won't be riding together."

"Aww," she says, disappointed. "We don't get to see each other that much as it is."

"You know how it is. It's training camp. But we're here right now, aren't we?"

"That's true, but I had to get fired to make it happen."

"That's not fucking true."

"Okay, okay. I guess I should just be happy with the fact that the great Rush Bacchetti is in my presence tonight," she mocks.

"Settle down."

Mia and I started on an equal playing field as student athletes in college, but now things are not so equal. It bothers me I'm the semi-famous one in this friendship with millions of dollars in the bank and Mia is a struggling physical therapist. Sometimes I even feel guilty about it.

I'm not saying that she would have ever had the same type of notoriety or income as a volleyball player, but she would have been an Olympic athlete. Her wish come true. And of course I can never forget or forgive myself that the one night she needed me, I wasn't there. By the time I found out what happened to her knee and arrived at the hospital, she was already under anesthesia and headed into exploratory surgery. She didn't even know I was there.

"Your modesty annoys me, Rush Bacchetti."

"Stop saying both of my names like that."

"Why?" She smiles a goofy grin. "That's your name, isn't it, Rush Bacchetti?"

"When will you get that I'm just a cog in the machine? The quarterback's ugly stepsister. I'm no Jett Caraway or Saint Stevenson."

"The quarterback position is overrated. It's all about the tight end. A very skilled position. You don't give yourself enough credit, best friend. Remember, no one thinks about Tom Brady without thinking about Gronkowski."

I smile reservedly and take a huge gulp of my cranberry juice. Mia is the only person besides my parents who can pay me a compliment, and I know there's no ulterior motive behind it. It's how she really sees me and that feels good, really good.

"I think you might just be my biggest fan, Bird."

"Always."

"Same."

My phone buzzes again, and I see it's Miranda. I respond to her text quickly, then copy and paste the information she's passed along to give to Mia.

"I'm sending you the info now," I tell her.

"For the job?"

"For the *interview*," I stress. Mia has an excitability about her and a way of jumping the gun on things. I, on the other hand, am a little more cautious. "The first one will be a phone interview."

"With the HR girl?"

"She's not a HR girl, she's a manager of the department,

and her name is Miranda. Miranda Green. Don't embarrass me and call her HR girl, okay?"

"*Ohhh*, Miranda, is it?" She says in a terrible Irish accent. Why she's picked, this accent is beyond me. Miranda is from the Bronx. "Do you have a thing going on with this Miranda woman?"

"No, Mia." I shake my head. "And why are you using that accent?"

"Did you have a thing with her?"

She won't stop with the accent.

It just hits me why.

She's tipsy and very soon on her way to drunk.

"We had a very brief thing a long time ago, and now we're cool."

"I knew it!"

"Don't let on that you are aware of that piece of information or you definitely won't get the job."

"I know how to act. Have I ever embarrassed you before?"

"Yes."

She slaps one of her palms against the table and laughs out loud.

"You're right. I've embarrassed you a million times."

Half of the bar turns around to stare at us after her outburst.

"A million and fucking one."

NINE

RUSH

THIS SPOT MUST BE full of single women tonight, because there is yet another woman who has been staring down my throat since Mia left the table to sing. She takes a full fifteen minutes to get her confidence up, but now she's finally making her approach. In a tight little black dress and heels, she's definitely overdressed for the tavern but totally fuckable.

"Excuse me, I don't mean to interrupt your evening, but I just wanted to tell you that I think you're the best player the Hawks have ever had and I'm a huge fan."

I can feel Mia's judgmental energy without even looking at her. She's doesn't approve; probably because the first thing you can see are this woman's tits jiggling inside of her dress. That and the fact that she doesn't even acknowledge that I'm sitting at this table with Mia. It's like Mia's invisible. I hate it when fans do that shit and the women do it the most. If only they knew Mia is the brightest star in this whole entire place, not me.

"Thank you."

The woman smiles uncomfortably. She expected me to

say something more to her, but I'm a man of few words and I'm not interested in anything more. I've always been uncomfortable with this type of attention, even when the woman is beautiful. It's just not the way I prefer to meet someone. I typically sleep with women I know through a mutual acquaintance or work like Miranda.

"So, um, that's all I wanted to say. Enjoy your evening."

She looks directly at Mia. "I'm sorry if I've interrupted."

"No problem," she tells the woman. "It happens all the time."

The woman walks away with a disappointed look on her face, but what did she expect? Don't I deserve to hang out with a friend for a night and not be interrupted by people who always want something from me?

"That was awkward," Mia quips.

"You made it awkward."

"Maybe I did with the last chick who had the nerve to ask if I was your sister, but not that one. I was on my best behavior just now. Your whole hot but silent act made it awkward."

"You think I'm hot?"

She's never said that before.

"The cluckers think you're hot, and that's all that matters."

"I wish you'd stop calling every woman who talks to me a clucker. Not all of them are gold diggers or sex addicts."

"Then why don't you talk to any of them?"

"I'm here with you."

"Yeah, but I'm not going home with you and getting in your bed tonight."

I shift uncomfortably in my seat at the image those words conjure up. I need my dick to settle the fuck down.

Mia is not someone for us to get excited over, dude.

"I'm not hurting for company if that's what you're worried about," I tell her.

"Oh."

"I mean, I don't tell you about every woman that I sleep with, Mia. That would just be weird."

"Why would it be weird?"

"They're just casual relationships. When something serious happens, you'll be the first to know."

Mia takes a sip of her vodka and cranberry, then completely pivots the conversation around back to her.

"So what should I wear for the first interview?"

"I told you it's a phone interview."

She pauses for a moment.

"Did you tell the HR lady about my knee?"

"Her name's Miranda."

"Right, did you tell *Miranda* about my knee?"

"No, did you want me to?"

"Um, I think I will need to mention it. There's no point in them wasting their time if they aren't interested in someone like me."

"As long as you can do the job, it shouldn't matter. It's against the law to not hire you based on your disability."

Shit, I didn't mean to say that. She hates it when I use that word.

"I'm not disabled."

Now she's using an awful British accent.

God help me.

"I don't know the politically correct way to say it, Mia."

"It's not about being *bloody* politically correct, it's about being accurate. I'm not always going to have a limp, so I'm not disabled."

"I know."

"This is a temporary situation."

Again with the accent. If someone from the United Kingdom is in this bar, they are going to be truly offended.

"Have you been watching *The Crown* again?"

"I just need another surgery by the right surgeon and I'll be good as new."

"Which I told you I'd pay for."

"Stop trying to give me all your money, Richie Rich. You're going to need it when you can't play ball anymore."

"I could stop playing ball tomorrow and still have enough money to pay for your surgery."

"Okay, now that was obnoxious."

Her American accent and attitude are back.

"Fine," I sigh. "You have to do everything the hard way, don't you?"

"Ha, you sound like the last dude I dated."

Mia unexpectedly stands, leans over the table and gives me a kiss on the cheek. Right above the fresh scar on my face.

"If I didn't say it before, thank you for tonight and the call you made on my behalf. I won't ever forget it."

I ignore the collective gasp in the bar as they watch the interaction between us. I think someone may have even snapped a picture. Mia has always been a touchy-feely kind of person. When the spirit moves her, she just has to act, and I definitely didn't mind it.

"What did I tell you about thanking me?"

"It's hard not to. You're just so awesome."

"Well, try harder." I smirk.

"I bet you'd do anything to cheer me up tonight, wouldn't you?"

This can't be headed anywhere good.

"Mia–"

"This is probably the second crappiest day of my life. I

need cheering up."

"I thought that's what I've been doing all night."

"I need more. I'm greedy. I want *you* to sing."

"No way."

"It's karaoke night."

"Hell, no, Mia."

Her persuasive smile (Mia has an arsenal of irresistible grins) spreads all the way to her doe brown, almond-shaped eyes.

"Please?"

I exhale with disapproval. I have zero interest in singing in public. She's taking advantage of me because she knows I won't tell her no. I never tell Mia no... not and truly mean it.

"Fuck, Mia. Fine. What song do you have in mind?"

"Yess!!!" She uses a fist cheer. "Tonight we're both going to sing *Bohemian Rhapsody* together. I need you to do the low parts and I'll take the high. The crowd in here will love it. We'll get a standing ovation."

"I don't know that song."

"Stop lying, everyone knows *Bohemian Rhapsody*."

"Seriously, crazy woman, not everyone knows it."

"You'll learn."

Thirty minutes later, we're deep in our second round of drinks, an order of hot wings, and a room full of people singing Bohemian Rhapsody along with us.

I learned the low parts in record time.

We were both awful and off-key, but that didn't matter to me, because I'm pretty sure I helped turn what was one of the lowest days Mia's had in a very long time into a good one.

And oddly enough, it was a blast.

Which is all I ever have when I'm with her.

Pure, unadulterated, fun.

TEN

MIA

INTERVIEWING with a pro ball team like the New York Nighthawks is a process, even when you have an inside track with the decision makers. After several email exchanges with staff members in the human resources department, it was explained to me I would be applying for a position made vacant by a beloved team therapist who retired to take care of his ailing wife. In other words, I'd have big shoes to fill if I were to get the position.

No sweat.

I eat challenges for breakfast.

Before my phone interview, I am directed to complete an extensive online application including a detailed educational background, job history and personal statement. I decided to bite the bullet and use the personal statement section to explain my injury and how it hasn't hindered me from performing my job.

After a few days of anxiously biting my nails, I was contacted again via email and was scheduled today for a preliminary phone interview (as he promised) with Rush's friend in HR who is probably screening me to see if I'm worth passing off to the actual decision makers in the department.

I have a million questions about the other therapists on staff, the hours, and the players that I wish I knew the answers to prior to this interview, but I didn't want to grill Rush about those things because he's already gone above and beyond the call of friendship to hook this whole thing up.

I'm also a bit conflicted that this is a phone interview. While I explained myself in the application, Miranda will not see me to be assured that my leg is a non-issue.

For some athletes, a torn ACL can heal with proper medical attention and rest, but after two excruciating surgeries and a long recovery, my leg has never completely healed. I'm one of the unlucky ones. What's wack-a-doodle about my injury is that there are some days that I don't need my cane, and then there are other days when I feel like I might fall on my ass if I try to take a step without it.

The inconsistency of my pain can sometimes appear as if it isn't real or as if I'm faking it. One day I'm walking fairly normally and another day I rather just sit. At my old job, my injury almost faded into the background. No one talked about it and it was never a hinderance to my work, but today I'm reminded just how much my life has been impacted by my knee.

I'm frightened that I'll never get hired again.

And getting this job would be the dream.

The new dream.

Rush told me that Miranda was tough but fair, so all I can do is play the interview by ear and hope for the best.

"Afternoon, Miss Taylor."

"Good afternoon, Miss Green."

"Is it okay if I call you Mia?"

"I'd prefer it, thank you."

"Great, and you can call me Miranda. So, Mia, I'm on a tight schedule today so let's just jump in if you don't mind."

Okay, so we're done with the pleasantries.

"That's fine with me."

"Perfect. So I reviewed your resume and see that you received your Master's degree in PT from Phoenixville University."

"That's correct."

"And you're state certified?"

"Yes."

"And you worked there for over four years, is that correct?"

"Yes."

"So may I ask why you are leaving?"

"I was laid off because of university budget cuts."

"That's a shame, but they gave you a glowing reference. You seemed to have left quite an impression."

"I enjoyed my time there."

"And you worked with football players?"

"I was fortunate enough to have a paid residency there my first year of graduate school, and I worked with athletes in a variety of sports. Then the next year and beyond I worked solely with Phoenixville's football program. Because of that opportunity, I was able to work with athletes with acute injuries and follow their cases all the way from rehab to recovery, so I think I can bring a unique viewpoint to the job."

"You're quite young, Mia. The athletes at the university were probably younger than you, and most of the players you'd be working with in the NFL are your age or older. Does that intimidate you at all?"

"It's my job to get each client back to where they need

to be in order to play at their optimal best regardless of the age of who I'm dealing with. It won't be an issue."

"And the fact that you're a woman?"

"Is a non-factor. I will come to work as a staff therapist and a skilled clinician. It won't hinder my productivity and I won't need any special treatment, nor do I want it."

My nerves are finally settling. I'm growing more confident with each exchange. I may not be the NFL's typical candidate for a position like this, but I know my stuff, so I take comfort in that.

I hear Miranda momentarily type some notes on a keyboard, and then she continues with the interview.

"Imagine this scenario, Mia. A player is injured during a game and protocol requires four weeks of therapy, but he pushes you to clear him in two because he wants to play. What do you do?"

"Player health is my number one priority. I would explain the risks to the player and if he still pushed, I would have no choice but to defer to my immediate superior. I will not clear anyone who I don't think is ready."

"Speaking of the Director of Rehab and PT for the Nighthawks, his name is Scott Maxwell. He's a straight shooter and a great clinician from what I hear around the office. You'd be working with him, two other full-time physical therapists, three strength and conditioning trainers and three athletic training interns."

A full staff.

"That's awesome."

"You'd be jumping in head first if we offer you the position. Training camp has already started, and it's basically a seven-day grind during this time of year. It's no cakewalk."

"I look forward to it. I enjoy keeping busy."

"Mmm hmm."

She types again.

"Just a couple more things, Mia."

"Sure."

"I have over seven qualified applicants interested in this position, and the reality is that most of them are more seasoned than you. All of them are dual certified like yourself but have years more experience. The only thing they're missing is the connection that got you this interview."

I gulp nervously.

I knew this was bound to come up, but I didn't think she'd be so direct about it. This Miranda woman is exactly like Rush described.

Tough.

ELEVEN

MIA

"You know Rush Bacchetti," she says in an almost accusatory way.

"Yes, I do."

"He seems to think that you're extremely capable of doing this job. In fact, he thinks we'd be making a terrible mistake if we took you out of the running just because of your age and work experience."

"That was very kind of him to say, and I humbly must agree with him. I love the sport just as much as anyone, I'd be easy to train because I'm not used to another team's system, and at the end of the day I'm a damn good clinician."

Yikes, maybe I shouldn't have said the word damn. Sometimes I get too passionate about things for my own good. I try taking the foot out of my own mouth.

"What I'm trying to say is that there's a fresh and progressive prospective I think I'll bring to the job and if you really want the truth, I make friends easily which is the key to successful treatment. When players feel as if they have a connection with their therapist, they are more apt to follow the treatment plan designed for them."

"Mmm, okay."

She types again, then asks her next question quite seriously.

"May I ask if the two of you are romantically involved?"

"You mean with Rush?" I practically scoff.

"Yes. I'm not trying to pry into your personal affairs, but decision makers will want to know if you're in some sort of romantic relationship with one of the players."

Decision makers like herself, I bet.

Miranda definitely still has the hots for Rush.

"We currently are not nor ever have been in that type of relationship," I assure her. "He's basically like the brother I never had."

"Then I think that's all I need, Mia. I want to say that it's been a pleasure talking to you today and good luck to you. It would be lovely to see another woman on staff."

"I was wondering where do we go from here?"

"I have to discuss our conversation and my notes with my superiors, but I'll be the one who lets you know what the next steps are."

"Sounds good. Thank you for the opportunity and have a great day."

"You as well."

***

The next day, after a rousing forty-two minutes of singing the entire Michael Jackson *Thriller* album in the shower, I slather some vanilla scented, deep conditioner on my hair, put it up in a bun, and check emails.

Even though I think I had what was a pretty good

initial interview with Miranda for the job, I still have several other irons in the fire with local practices and hope to hear about an interview with one of them soon. These bills aren't going to pay themselves and time is ticking.

My cell phone rings, and my chest tightens with anxiety. It's my mother, and I know exactly why she's calling.

"Hi, Mandy."

"Are you busy, Mia?"

"It's hair day so a little."

"I didn't get a check from you this month."

"Oh, I ran out of checks," I fib. "And I don't use them enough to justify the cost of ordering more."

"So that means you're not going to pay your bills?"

"Of course not. You'll get it."

"The tax payment is due at the end of next week. No later. We're already past the first deadline," she huffs. "Now there's a late fee."

"Can you give me the mailing address? I'll have the bank issue me a check and I'll send it directly."

"No, you can send it to me as usual. It might be better if you send me the money with one of those apps everyone is using now. You just have to walk me through how to set it up."

Mandy has never been easy and is exactly why I am extremely motivated to never return home and live with her. She is forcing me into a corner and I can't stall any longer. I'm going to have to tell her.

"I'm going to need a little more time."

"Time? I thought it was about not having a check."

"I'm running short this month."

"You make twice what I do and you're running short?

What are you spending your money on up there, Broadway shows and cabs?"

"The cost of living is higher here. I have a lot of bills."

"Then bring your narrow ass back home and help me share the bills of this monstrosity of a house your grandmother left us."

"My job is here."

Correction, my job *was* here.

"You should have never bought that high-end car. You obviously can't afford it."

"I bought the Prius used and I wouldn't say that it's high-end, just energy efficient."

"I'm sure it costs more than my monthly bus fare to my job, so in my opinion, it's high-end and was a stupid purchase."

"This from a woman who spends half her paycheck on cartons of Newports," I blurt out.

"What did you just say to me?"

"I didn't–"

"I raised your little ungrateful ass, Mia Taylor, when I didn't have to. I put clothes on your back and made sure you had three squares to eat when your father didn't give a damn."

That's exactly not how I remember it.

"I'll get you the money," I say flatly. "I'm sure Grandma is watching and worried."

"What the hell is that supposed to mean?"

I've made Mandy upset. I can hear her taking a deep puff of one of her cigarettes to calm herself down, and no matter how I feel about her questionable mothering skills, I can't help but to feel guilty. She is my mother, after all. I owe her some degree of respect.

"I just meant that I don't want to let Grandma down."

"Get back to your hair and I'll talk to you later. Text me once you've sent the check out."

"Bye, Mandy."

She hangs up on me without a proper farewell.

Yeah, she's angry.

I go back to scrolling through emails wishing like hell I could have a do-over of that conversation. Mandy pushes all of my buttons and I know how to push hers. It isn't good for either of us. I'm considering all the ways I might stall the creditors of my other bills to get her the tax payment when I get an alert for an email that changes everything.

To: Mia Taylor
From: Miranda Green
Re: PT Position

Dear Miss Taylor,

We are pleased to offer you a position with The New York Nighthawks as a full-time staff physical therapist in the Rehab and PT Department effective immediately.

We feel that with your skills and qualifications, you will be a valuable addition to our department. Your starting date will be Monday, July 9. The starting annual salary with our organization is $76,266, and you are paid on a bi-monthly basis.

The attached employee handbook outlines the medical and retirement benefits The New

York Nighthawks offers. Benefits would begin upon acceptance of this offer.

If you choose to accept this offer, please wet sign the second copy of this letter in the space provided and return it to us immediately. We hope you will accept this offer of employment and look forward to welcoming you as a new employee of the Nighthawks family.

Sincerely,

Miranda Green

Human Resources

New York Nighthawks

What in the ever loving fuck?!

I got a job offer in less than twenty-four hours with the New York Nighthawks.

Holy crap, I'm rich!

I've gotta call Rush.

I know for certain that my lucky charm had something to do with this. What on earth would I do without that man?

I just pray that I never, ever have to find out.

TWELVE

MIA

I'm not that great of a cook, but there are very few ways to thank a millionaire when you're on a limited budget, so I've invited Rush over for a home cooked meal for the first time in our friendship. It might not be the best thing he's ever eaten, but there will be plenty of it, and if there's one thing I know about him, it's that he can consume an enormous amount of chow in one sitting.

"Hey."

"Hey, yourself."

"Shit, is that blood on your face, Bird?"

He leans over to swipe the "blood" from under my eye with the pad of his thumb.

Oddly, my stomach flutters when he touches my face. I guess I'm nervous that he's seeing the inside of my new apartment for the first time. I've been here less than a year, but he's been out of town a lot for football.

"No," I awkwardly back away from his hand. "It's just sauce."

If he's confused by my reaction, he quickly shrugs it off

and enters my apartment, filling the small space with his massive body and formidable presence.

Rush is wearing an official Nighthawks black t-shirt with the team logo in the center, dark wash jeans, and a pair of his favorite black combat boots. If I didn't know him to be the calm, gentle giant that he is, I'd be scared shitless of all tattooed, six feet five inches of him.

"You've got some sort of weird emotional attachment to those boots if you ask me. Take 'em off," I demand. "You know the rules. They're the same in every apartment. I'm anal about keeping the floors clean and God knows what the treads of your boots have stepped on."

"My boots are clean, but whatever you say, hard ass."

I give him a quick squeeze around the waist.

"I hope you're hungry," I tell him. "You smell good. What are you wearing?"

He smells extra divine tonight. Must be the perks of being able to afford such expensive cologne and aftershave.

"Soap and water."

"Aww, you took a shower just for me?"

"Funny."

He tosses a plastic shopping bag hard toward my chest that I catch like the volleyball queen that I still am.

"What's this?"

"Look inside."

I scream once I pull it out.

"Oh my God!"

It's an official throwback Saint Stevenson football jersey with his autograph on the back.

"You like?"

"I love it! You know he was my favorite player of all time."

"I thought I was your favorite."

"After you, of course," I say as I slide the jersey on top of my clothes. "Ooh, it's so roomy."

I pose like a model in front of the simple tall mirror affixed on the wall next to my door.

"It was the jersey he wore the last time he won the division. I couldn't get you a Super Bowl one because he auctions those for charity."

"He actually wore this?" I pull at the material and sniff it. "I think an actual tear of joy just fell from my eye."

"It's your congratulations gift for becoming an official Nighthawk. Welcome to the team."

Rush takes a moment to look around my small one-bedroom apartment.

"So this is your famous new bachelorette pad?"

"Yep."

I spread my arms wide and slowly twirl.

"How do you like it?"

"It's totally you."

Rush crashes his heavy body on the blue couch I bought for a steal in the Ikea As-Is section, and the joints of it make a squeaky cry for help. It's the only half-decent piece of furniture I own, but it's probably going to need replacing soon.

"Take it easy, big boy. I think you may just break my precious couch if you're not careful."

"A simple summer breeze from your window could break this precious couch."

"Very funny, Bacchetti. Not all of us can afford hand-carved Italian furniture flown in from the motherland."

He rolls his eyes.

"What's for dinner? Smells good."

"A Taylor family specialty."

"Which is?"

"Spaghetti and meatballs, salad, and garlic bread. The meatballs are made with a combination of ground lamb and beef."

"Impressive."

"I know, right? Since I'm not allowed to say the forbidden words between us, I thought the next best thing would be to cook you a celebration dinner."

"You better take that jersey off then. I don't want you getting any Taylor family sauce on it. It's a collector's item."

I cock my head to side. "How much did this cost you?"

"I'm not telling."

"You didn't get it for free?"

"No, Bird. Stevenson doesn't just give away his jerseys to random people for free."

"You're not random." I shake my head and feign disappointment. "When are you going to realize that you are the most feared, most talented, tight end in the league?"

"You should start a fan club for me," he jests.

I know that I often make Rush uncomfortable with my compliments because he isn't your typical vain football star. He knows he's talented, but he doesn't like a fuss to be made about it. He's always been that way. But that doesn't mean I'm going to allow him to forget who he is to this game... a freakin' phenom.

"I would start the Bacchetti fan club, but then I'd make everyone sing *Purple Rain* as a requirement to get in. They'd hate it."

"I like Prince and even I'd hate that," he quips.

I pull off my gift with the quickness and hang it carefully in my closet. I have a feeling I could auction it at Sotheby's in ten years and buy a beach house with the proceeds, so I better take good care of it.

"I can't believe you got this for me," I say, overwhelmed by his generosity.

"I can't believe you actually got the job."

"Stop the act, Bacchetti. It's obvious that you had everything to do with me getting the job so quickly."

"I swear I had nothing to do with it. They wanted to fill the spot ASAP."

"Yeah, but she said that she needed to pass her notes to her superiors. There's no way she did all of that in twenty-four hours."

"Actually, it's very possible that she did. They work fast and well past the usual nine-to-five hours."

"I guess I have a lot to learn about how the NFL works."

"I'm just trying to figure out what the hell you said to Miranda in that interview. She must really like you. I heard she's an especially unyielding interviewer."

"You heard? Give me a break. Don't you already know? I thought you and your lady friend would have discussed all types of things by now."

"My lady friend, Mia?" He sounds exasperated.

"Miranda is a lady, and she is your friend. Your friend with benefits." I wiggle my eyebrows.

"I told you before that our days of *benefits* were a long time ago."

"She seems nice enough, Rush. Normal. She has a good job and a sexy phone voice. I wouldn't object to you two going on another date."

"Thanks, I'll keep that in mind," he says snidely.

I walk over and stir my pot of sauce. It smells damn good if I say so myself. I even diced an onion and a green pepper and tossed them in there like Grandma used to do.

"Do you think it's odd that she didn't bring up my knee

during the interview and then offered me the position so quickly?"

"Is that why you think I had something to do with it?"

"Don't you think it's unusual?"

"Did you bring your knee up to her?" he asks reservedly, as if he's walking onto a landmine.

"I didn't find the right time."

"You didn't even mention it once?"

"Dude, I was kind of nervous. I said the word damn by mistake and I think she was worried about my age and length of work experience, so I didn't want to offer up any more strikes against me on a silver platter."

"Your leg was kind of a big thing to leave out, Bird."

"I didn't technically leave it out. I included it on my application."

"Oh, well, you should have led with that. If you mentioned on there, then you're good and the bottom line is you got the job, so there's no need for us to speculate about it anymore."

"Just humor me a little longer. Why didn't you tell her about the knee when you recommended me?"

Rush stalks over to me, probably annoyed with the length and direction of this topic of conversation, and then the oddest thing happens. He strokes the smooth hairs of my ponytail back in the most intimate and calming way.

"Because it's your story to tell, Bird."

Rush maintains unwavering and intense eye contact with me, and all I can hear are the labored breaths between us. For a moment, it almost feels like he's going to kiss me.

But then my sauce bubbles over.

"Oops, dinner's ready," I say in a small voice to break the erotic tension between us.

He nods in a way that disconcerts me. Like he's saying *until next time* in a sinister Darth Vader voice.

"Okay, Bird."

His feet stay planted in place, which forces me to slip around his body and start serving dinner. I place two large serving bowls of pasta and green salad on my retro glass coffee table that I purchased from a consignment shop. Rush follows over to the table and starts making his plate while I return to the kitchen to grab the garlic bread out of the oven. I practically feel like I'm running from him in my own house.

"When do you start?" he asks as if nothing bizarre just happened between the two of us.

"My first day is Monday. I think they want to fill the position quickly because of training camp."

"Yeah, camp is brutal. It's seven days a week, but then things slow down once preseason starts. We get days off then."

"All I'm doing on Monday is meeting my boss, going for a tour of the training facilities, and filling out paperwork."

He turns his head to stare at me at the stove, but his eyes land right on my butt and linger there.

"Are you looking at my ass?" I try joking with him to add some levity back into the evening.

His eyes dart away uncomfortably.

"Of course not."

"Of course not?" I dramatically glance down at my butt. "What's wrong with my ass?"

"Nothing's wrong with it," he huffs.

"Then why of *course* not?"

"Mia."

"What?"

"You have a beautiful ass."

My stomach flutters after he pays me the compliment. It shouldn't but it does. It's only Rush, but there's something about his approval and admiration that makes my heart sing a rift.

Maybe it's because he doesn't give compliments often, which gives them so much more meaning.

Or maybe it's because something is changing between us.

Something for the life of me I can't explain.

THIRTEEN

RUSH CLEARS his throat and swiftly changes the subject.

"So do you have to come to training camp every day once you start?"

I give him a look like he's bumped his head too many times on the turf.

"Obviously, duh. Where else am I going to work with the players?"

"Right, that was a dumb question."

He turns back around and picks up the remote.

"So what are we watching?" he asks in a clipped tone.

He's acting weird suddenly. Let me rephrase that, *weirder*. I sit down at the opposite end of my tiny couch and start making my plate.

"I don't know, maybe something with a superhero."

He silently starts flicking through the channels looking for an action flick to watch and mindlessly goes right past the first *Thor* movie.

"Hey, go back a few channels. You totally breezed right by Thor."

"You want to watch that movie again?"

"Is that even a real question?"

His mouth flattens into a thin line as he goes back to the right movie channel.

"Dude, what's wrong with you?" I finally ask, hoping he will fix his face. We had a weird minute but it's over.

"Everything's fine, Bird. It's just that things are a little tense at work."

I have to laugh at myself.

I thought things were weird because he almost kissed me, but that wasn't it at all. It's work stuff. Of course. Rush has little time to be concerned about anything else.

"A few of the guys are having a conflict and it's spilling over into the locker room. I didn't realize that you'd be starting the job this soon. I just hope everyone will be on their best behavior when they work with you. I don't want you to get hurt."

"*Ohhh*, so that's where you got the gash on your face?"

He nods.

"Don't worry, I've worked with rowdy athletes for years. It'll be fine. I'm not new at this."

"You've worked with rowdy *college* players. These are grown ass men who sometimes don't know their own strength. I was just in an all-out brawl with some of them not that long ago."

"I'm sure that was a fluke."

"And with your knee situation–"

"It's all about good body mechanics in a PT room," I cut him off. "And I promise to use my cane on the days I need to. I won't hide it. I promise. You worry too much, *paw-paw*. Now mix up your salad. The dressing and some cucumbers may have sunken to the bottom."

He sighs and shovels a fork full of the mixed green salad in his mouth. Rush doesn't like his food to touch and only eats things on his plate one food group at a time in order of least favorite to most. Vegetables are eaten first, carbs second, and then he'll save the meatballs for last. It's a quirky but cute thing about him. We always used to argue in college when I wanted to order a half-plain and half-Hawaiian pizza because they would inevitably put a few pineapple chunks too close to his plain slices.

He still doesn't look convinced, and I try to think of some comforting words to snap him out of this sudden sour mood. It feels as if he's already regretting referring me for this job, and I can't allow that to come between us.

"I understand your sudden reluctance. These are your friends. Your colleagues. You don't want me breaking out in song in the training room or falling on my ass in front of them."

"I'm not saying that at all, Mia. You're missing the point. Forget I said anything."

I squint my eyes as I take a bite of one of my meatballs. Dammit, I put too much oregano or something in them.

"Don't worry so much. It's going to be great. You and I will work at the same place, I'm starting work mid-pay-cycle so I'll get paid next week, and my health benefits kick in on the first day of employment. No probationary period. I can keep my appointment with the ortho surgeon. This job is the gift that keeps on giving, and I will not let you put a damper on it with your worrying."

"Fine, I'm done talking about it."

"You're done like you're sick of me or done like we're good."

"We're good, Bird. We're always good."

I stop chewing for a moment in solemn appreciation of Thor as his fine ass flashes on the screen.

"God, that man is amazing."

"You do realize that's computer-generated imagery making the actor look larger than life."

"That is an absolute falsity. Each and every one of those muscles is real because one, the internet says so and two, I can tell. I work with athletic physiques for a living. Just like how I know your guns are real."

I lean over and pat one of his ripped biceps, and Rush cracks a smile.

"You think I look like Thor?"

"I think you could easily be Chris Hemsworth's Hollywood body double with the right blonde wig, of course."

"The food's good, Bird." He grins as he heartily shovels in a forkful of his pasta next. "It tastes damn near like my Mom's."

My best friend has finally shown back up.

Weirdness gone.

Maybe he just needed a compliment to make his heart sing too.

"Good, I'm glad you like it."

I lift my bad leg and prop it up on my bean bag stool.

"Is it hurting badly today?" He sounds concerned as he gently rubs the supporting muscles around my knee for me.

"I think it's going to rain tonight. That's probably why I ache. I should be fine by Monday."

"Good."

Rush polishes off the rest of his meal, finally ending with my over-seasoned meatballs, then stretches out on the couch, and pivots me around so that he can position my bum leg on top of his thighs.

Twenty-five minutes later I'm deep into a movie that I could recite line for line and Rush is deep in REM sleep.

His long eyelashes flutter as he twitches.

And both of his enormous hands still cradle my leg.

It's not like I didn't know it already, but good gravy he's handsome.

Whoever the woman is, that eventually lands my bestie, is going to be one lucky mother clucker.

FOURTEEN

FIRST DAY AT TRAINING CAMP

"World domination greetings, Mia."

"World domination greetings, Rush."

"Talk to you after you kick ass at your new job today?"

"Affirmative."

It's always been my job to help athletes either train to stay in prime physical condition or to help them rehab after an injury, so most of the time I wear sweats. There's not one day I'm not in a pair of sweatpants and a zipped hoodie. In fact, I don't think I've been in real clothes since my Uncle John's funeral. That's why I've decided that for my first day of work, which is only going to involve a tour and paperwork, I will dress the part of a professional.

I wear a scoop neck, sleeveless, green silk blouse (my favorite color) with a dark green pencil skirt and white blazer that skims my tall and bootylicious frame perfectly. I flat iron and then smooth my medium-length hair back in a smooth ponytail, neatly braiding it and securing the end with a small black rubber band. I can no longer wear heels because of my knee, so I choose a pair of crisp white Converse that dresses the outfit down and makes me look less corporate and more NFL cool chick. Then I top the whole thing off with the two-carat diamond stud earrings Rush bought me the first Christmas after he signed with the Nighthawks.

I look good if I do say so myself.

Today's drive in the green goblin is all about hype music. My playlist is 90s hip hop featuring the Wu-Tang Clan as I travel twenty-five minutes to the team's summer training camp facilities a few towns over in Central New Jersey. I am admittedly excited about today for a lot of reasons, but feel totally centered since Rush called me this morning with our traditional pregame pep call.

Once I arrive, I'm directed to a large parking garage where there is plenty of close parking to the elevator. When I exit, I notice there's a striking woman with a lavender-dyed bob and dressed in an all white track suit waiting for me in a golf cart.

"Mia?"

"Miranda?"

"Yes, it's a pleasure to meet you."

She is nothing like I imagined her to be. She looks like one of those cute girls that works at the cool T-shirt store in the mall, not a high-powered NFL Human Resources executive. I can see why Rush was sleeping with her. She's absolutely gorgeous, totally badass, and I'm majorly intimidated.

Miranda stares at my cane for a moment and then back at me.

"Welcome to Nighthawk's camp."

I turn my head around and take in all the awesomeness of this moment.

"Thanks! The campus is gorgeous."

"We have more ground to cover today, so I brought the golf cart. No need to mess up a perfectly good pair of sneakers if we don't have to. The ground is still soft from the rain the other day."

"Perfect."

I'm grateful for the ride because now that I look at the vast size of the training campus, there's probably no way I could have walked the entire way without slowing Miranda down. The distance from the field to the training buildings is quite long, and for a brief moment I second guess my ability to physically do this job.

Have I overestimated the task?

Am I setting myself up for failure?

My doubts slowly dissipate and my eagerness to learn the job blossoms as Miranda continues to show me around camp.

"The Nighthawks have been getting ready for the season in this facility for over fifteen years. We make regular updates and modifications to the buildings, and all of our equipment is state-of-the art. You'll find that our training facility rivals most NFL teams' camps."

I've worked with athletes for many years as a student and now as a therapist, but there is a level of professionalism and privilege here that is beyond what I've ever experienced. This is why working for a pro team is the "new" dream. I feel like I'm going to be quickly forced to step up my game and I look forward to it.

I notice small groups of players running various drills on the field, which reminds me of a question to ask Miranda.

"I see they practice on real grass. Does that make a difference in the amount of turf toe or high ankle sprain injuries that you see when the season starts and they play on artificial turf in other cities?"

Miranda looks impressed by my question.

"Honestly, I don't know the answer to that," she admits. "Scott and the rest of the team you'll be working with will have those answers. Be sure to ask him."

Scott is my immediate supervisor, but I haven't met him yet. The NFL works very differently than my previous employer. I would have never been hired at Phoenixville without interviewing with my supervisor first, but I guess that's how things work on this level.

"Let's go meet Scott now."

A few heads turn as we drive the golf cart towards the main training building.

"Don't mind them," Miranda says. "They're harmless. They just don't see that many women out here so they can't help but stare."

"I can't wait for the day when seeing women on the field will be uneventful. Soon, it'll be commonplace to see female therapists, trainers and coaches in the NFL," I comment.

"If it's going to happen, then I'm sure it will be with the Nighthawks. We have a very progressive owner. It's part of the reason why we hired you."

Oh, that makes sense. Being a woman could be the one advantage I had over all the rest of the candidates. I'll never know for sure, but I think that's what Miranda is hinting at.

"I've read that about Mr. Parker. It's good to know that there is truth to the stories that he's looking to make progressive changes in the league. Do you think I'll ever meet him?"

"Mr. Parker is pretty hands-on, but the truth is if we win, then you may meet him, but if we have a losing season, you definitely won't."

I grow a little nervous when we get to the training center. My knee feels great today and I rather not attract any extra attention by carrying my cane with me, so I leave it in the cart. Honestly, I should have never taken it out of the car to begin with, but it's habit at this point.

Miranda notices but still doesn't address it, no doubt being respectful of my privacy. I like her even more because of that. I'm going to have to have a long conversation with Rush about her later. I want to know the real scoop about these two.

We walk in what feels like a labyrinth of hallways and rooms. There are designated areas for every treatment you could imagine: steam rooms, acupuncture area, ice bath room, massage section, strength training room, cardio area. The place is massive and a therapist's dream. There is room to execute a complicated treatment plan here without having to step all over each other's toes like we did at my old job.

We arrive to the main physical therapy room where I'm to meet my coworkers.

"Hey, Scott, can you come here for a second?"

My new supervisor is a buff man, about six-feet-tall with ice-blue eyes and silver hair that's effortlessly slicked back. He's stretching out a player I don't recognize.

"This is the newbie?"

"Scott, this is Mia Taylor. Mia, this is the senior PT here, Scott Maxwell."

We shake hands.

His hand is kind of sweaty and it takes everything for me not to slide it down the side of my skirt to wipe it off.

"Nice to meet you, Mia."

"Nice to meet you."

"You handing her over to me, Miranda?"

"For a few. Then she'll need to handle paperwork with me."

"Cool. Ok, kiddo, you're with me for an hour. I'm stretching out Darius. Come on over and meet him."

I'm growing more excited about things. I'm meeting players already, and Scott seems easy to work with.

"Awesome, I'll see you later, Miranda."

She smiles. "I'll be back around lunchtime."

Before she walks off she pauses a moment then asks, "Do you need your things out of the golf cart?"

"Um, no. I'm fine."

"Ok." She nods and then walks off. Her blunt cut bob of lavender hair swinging behind her.

"Darius, this is Mia, our new PT. She's going to help stretch you out. Mia, Darius injured his left hamstring at the end of last season. He's almost as good as new, but we're going to baby it for a while longer because he's a starter this season."

Man, I didn't realize that they'd throw me right into some actual work today, but if women used to ride horses side saddle, then I can definitely stretch out one player in a pencil skirt.

"Nice to meet you, Mia," Darius says in a flirty way. He's probably a year or so younger than me, but he's also twice my size, so it's important for me to stabilize my body so that I can leverage my weight properly when I stretch his leg.

"Hey, Darius, ready to get this leg feeling better?"

"Ready, Freddy."

There are thick cushioned pads on the floor, much like the ones you'd see in a gymnast's studio. Darius is lying in the middle of it on his back. I'm going to have to be careful on this padding. The cushions can give underneath when you walk on them and I could lose my balance. I decide the best approach would be to slightly hike up my skirt and stabilize myself on my knees in front of his raised leg, then stretch it out by pushing it toward him.

It works.

I squeeze his hamstring muscle with my hand as I push his leg back to see just how tight it is. It's still pretty tight. Darius is going to have some work to do to be ready in time for the season. I hear the deep voices of several men in conversation enter the room behind me as I continue my work.

Upon approach, they stop talking.

Then they say only one word.

"Dayummmm!"

FIFTEEN

MIA

I should be irritated that some Nighthawks are already objectifying me, but even I have to admit that the scene they've walked in on probably looks a bit unusual. From their vantage point, a strange woman is on her knees, in a tight skirt that's hiked up, with her butt in the air in front of Darius. Definitely not the first impression I wanted to make. It would look completely different if I was in a team issued tracksuit.

"Damn, who is that Darius? That better not be your sister because I think I'm in love."

Darius smiles at me as Scott makes the awkward introductions.

"She's nobody's sister, Hampton. She's the new therapist here and you'll pay her the respect of everyone else on staff," Scott interjects firmly.

I think Scott and I are going to get along famously. He's no nonsense and obviously well respected. I turn my head to introduce myself properly and am surprised to find that Rush is a quiet part of the group of players who are staring at me like I'm a ham sandwich. We lock eyes and my face brightens like a Christmas tree. I'm so glad to see his grumpy-cute face.

"Damn, Scott. We're sorry. It was the pretty girl that threw us off. We didn't know she was staff. Nice to meet you, Mia, we're the tight ends on the team. I'm Barry Hampton, this is John Dixon, and this here is Rush Bacchetti."

Rush's face is rigid and silent.

Now that I think about it, things moved so fast and the two of us never discussed if I'm supposed to hide the fact that we are friends or what. I didn't think keeping it from his teammates was even a consideration, but now that I'm seeing how distant he's acting, I'm not so sure.

"Um, it's really nice to meet you all too. I look forward to working with you."

I realize I've had Darius's leg stretched a little too long and slowly lower it back to the ground. Then I sit back on my heels as three more men walk into the room. One I recognize as the new quarterback of the team and the other I think is an offensive player that Rush has mentioned in passing named Tiger Samuels.

I attempt to stand to greet everyone properly, but am a bit wobbly as the mat gives underneath my weight, just as I feared. I have nothing to hold on to to stabilize myself, but Samuels notices right away and makes a beeline straight for me, offering me his hand to stand up.

"Want some help?"

"Oh, thank you."

"I just overheard that you're the new PT?"

I can already tell that Tiger Samuels has a way about him. He's attractive, polite, chivalrous... and probably trouble. He has that All-American, I'm used to raising all sorts of hell look.

"Yes, I'm Mia."

"Please to meet you. I'm Tiger Samuels. Beacher and I were working together on strengthening my back. I have an old injury in the lower region from high school ball that needs constant strengthening, so I expect we'll work together at some point."

Samuels gives Scott a look as if he's asking for confirmation on that. Let's add the word assertive to the list of Samuel's way about him.

"This is her first day, Samuels. I haven't updated the schedule."

Rush is staring daggers at me or more specifically at Samuel's hold of my arm, then he breaks his silence and approaches us both.

"Are you all right?"

My eyes widen in reproach. I warned him about this. I don't want any unwanted attention paid to my knee, especially for my brand new boss to see.

"I'm fine."

Samuels and the rest of the room look confused as they watch our interaction unfold.

"Do you two know each other?" Samuels asks.

"Yes," Rush answers plainly with no other words for context.

"Oh." Samuels immediately lets go of my arm and his face appears solemn.

"We're friends from college," Rush declares suddenly.

"Oh, you're both Hurricanes?" Samuels asks.

"Yes." I add my two cents to the narrative. "Hurricanes for life."

After the group disperses to go to their assigned treatments, I finish working with Darius, meet the other therapists on staff (I am the only woman), and sit in on a mini meeting with them all. They are a well-oiled machine and have already decided what players on the roster I will start working with.

Darius is one.

Samuels and Rush are two others.

Miranda returns promptly by lunch to retrieve me to sign a mound of paperwork over a meal of shrimp caesar salad and unsweetened tea.

"So what did you think?" she asks.

"I think I'm going to love it here."

"That's good to hear. You seem to fit right in."

After a few silent chews of our food, Miranda asks me the question I think she's been dying to ask ever since this morning.

"So you and Rush."

"Yes?"

"You said you two are like brother and sister?"

I decide it would be best to continue with the underplayed truth Rush started in the training room.

"Well, we're college friends. Is there something you wanted to know?"

"I'm sorry for asking, it's just that, he never mentioned you."

I try not to let her words bother me, but they hurt. I'm pretty sure he slept with this woman on numerous occasions and it's obvious that she's no clucker, so why didn't he tell her about me?

There's a knock at the door that bails me out before I almost say something stupid.

"Who is it?"

"Bacchetti."

"His ears must have been burning," Miranda quips in a

very casual way, as if she's known Rush forever. "Come in, Rush."

He looks between the two of us, then his eyes finally land on mine.

"Can I talk to you for a minute, Mia?"

"Sure."

I get up slowly because my knee often aches if I've been sitting too long in one position, but then starts to loosen up once I get moving. Rush closes Miranda's door behind us and walks me toward the elevators, out of earshot.

"What's up?" I ask, still salty about what Miranda just shared.

"Why aren't you using your cane?"

"Because I don't need it today."

"You almost fell on top of Darius back there."

"But I didn't."

"And you're in this skirt? Who are you trying to impress?"

"It's my first day on the job and I wanted to look professional. I'm trying to impress every damn body!"

"You aren't a corporate fucking lawyer, you're a physical therapist. You should have worn sweats."

"And the last time I checked, my daddy is back in Pennsylvania, not in this hallway."

The nerve of him questioning me about my choices.

"I'm just looking out for you, Mia. The way I always have. The way I always will continue to do so."

"Are we supposed to be keeping our friendship a secret?" I blurt out. There's no need to beat around the bush.

"What?"

"Back there in the therapy room, I was so happy to see a

friendly face, but you barely acknowledged your college acquaintance."

I use air quotes.

"I never said the word acquaintance, and you played along with me."

"I was just following your lead."

"Well, you sold it well. Samuels seemed pleased."

"Samuels? Listen, do you want me to quit on my first day? I'm feeling like this job is going to be a huge inconvenience for you and your... other life."

Rush cracks the knuckles on his left hand. A telltale sign that this conversation is frustrating him, but I don't care. I'm freakin' frustrated too.

"What the fuck are you talking about, Bird. You're talking in riddles as usual. What other life?"

"Your pro football life. The life where no one knows who I am or that I even exist. I'm supposed to be your best friend and not one of those men in there ever heard of me and neither has Miranda."

"Miranda? Why would I tell her shit about the things or people who matter most to me?"

"Because you were sleeping with her?" I point and angrily whisper, remembering we are only a few feet away from her office.

"That doesn't have shit to do with anything."

"And that, ladies and gentleman, is what your problem is."

"What's my problem?" he asks through gritted teeth.

"You're closed off and you choose to compartmentalize your life like you're some sort of secret agent, never wanting one part to ever learn about the other."

He cracks his knuckles some more but doesn't respond.

"You have to let someone in eventually, Rush, and

Miranda seems like a really nice woman. No clucker tendencies whatsoever."

He walks closer toward me, and even though I'm relatively tall, he still towers over me by over six inches. His fiery eyes hold mine in rapt attention. His nostrils flare with emotion.

"Why do you keep talking about Miranda, Bird?"

"Because—"

"Do you want me to fuck her?"

"What?"

"I'm asking if it would make you happy if I fuck her, because I have no plans to.

The inside of my mouth feels dry and swollen, so I say nothing in response.

"Most of the time you're cock blocking any woman who gets near me, but suddenly you've never advocated so hard for me to fuck someone like you are her."

"Is that what you think I'm doing?"

"It's what I know you're doing and maybe you need to ask yourself why."

I barely stutter a response. Rush has never spoken to me this way before, and I'm not sure where it's coming from but that doesn't matter much right now, because Miranda is standing in the hallway close enough to hear us and the look on her face is haunting.

Imagine a puppy getting kicked in the face by a human it trusted and a human it loves.

I just wish the hallway would swallow me up whole.

What a shit first day.

SIXTEEN

RUSH

I TRAIN AGGRESSIVELY for the rest of the day in an effort to punish myself for my behavior. It's a bad habit I picked up from back in my high school days. I'm pissed mostly at myself because I reacted poorly today and hurt two women who didn't deserve it.

Miranda was completely embarrassed by my comments that she overhead and retreated back to her office as quickly as she appeared. I don't foresee us ever speaking again, and once Mia finishes her paperwork, I doubt she'll speak to her either.

I've been nervous from the start for Mia to take this job. She's the only woman in the PT department of an NFL team. She's single, statuesque, fit, and a gorgeous woman who men are undoubtedly going to hit on. What I didn't count on were my evolving feelings for her getting the way too.

Something is changing and I feel like captain obvious just gave me a hard elbow in the chest when I saw her chatting it up with Samuels. He's the last person on earth I need sniffing up under her ass. Just a second ago, he was fucking Proctor's mother. He's a self-indulgent, woman-obsessed asshole with no boundaries.

I don't want to shit talk one of my teammates to Mia, especially because she has to work with him, but I need to find a way to calmly squash this thing before it gets out of hand and I hurt someone. I think I just need a night to sleep on it and calm down.

I'm not the most strategic thinker when I'm angry, but perhaps fate has other plans for me today, because Samuels is headed directly my way and there can only be one thing he wants to talk to me about.

"You were fast as hell out there today," he says, blowing smoke completely up my ass.

"Yeah."

"So I just wanted to clear the air about Mia."

"What about her?"

My hackles rise.

"I realize she's your homegirl from college so I want to be respectful."

Fuck me.

"She's real hot and seems like a nice girl. I want to ask her out for a date."

"She's been working here for five hours and you want to ask her out already? That's working fast, even for you."

"Early bird gets the worm, man. If I don't ask her soon, somebody else is going to."

I hear ringing in my ears. There's a competition to get at Bird first? If this is what I have to look forward to for the rest of the season, I'm going to kill somebody and the most likely candidate today is Samuels.

"I rather you didn't," I tell him.

"Did you hit that in school or something?"

My blood is boiling.

"You're asking if I slept with her?" *Fuckhead.* "No, Samuels. She's... she's just a friend from school."

The half-truth I tell again tastes especially rancid, but I remember quickly why I'm saying it. It's all for Mia.

It's a shitty double standard, but the minute I act too protective over her, all kinds of incorrect assumptions are going to be made about our relationship. Many of them will assume we've slept together or that we are sleeping together. They will dismiss any of her accomplishments or credentials. The fact is that she needs to find her own place in the locker room without rumors or innuendo or she'll never be taken seriously.

"That's good news, but just so you know, my intentions are honorable. I'm just going to ask her out. No bullshit."

I take a deep calming breath because I really want to karate chop this fucker's windpipe.

"I'm asking you respectfully, Samuels, to wait on that. She barely got her foot in the door. It's a big deal for a woman to work on the training staff of any NFL team. She needs to make a good impression with no distractions or rumors."

"You make a good point, man. I should wait."

Maybe he's not a complete moronic, narcissistic jackass.

"You Hurricanes really stick together."

"Yeah, we do."

"But remember, I called first dibs."

"What the fuck does that mean?"

"I didn't mean it disrespectfully, Rush. I'm just saying I'm not going to ask her out today, but eventually I will, and I just want it on the record that I consulted you out of respect first since you know her and all."

"You're missing the point."

"Nah, man. I get exactly what you're saying. Before I

ask her out, I need to chill for a second. Good things come to those who wait. I got you."

After Samuels walks away, I take one of the practice balls and kick that shit down field. He doesn't get what I'm saying at all, or he doesn't want to get it. I'm realizing that there are so many reasons why Mia working for the NFL, especially on my team, was one of the dumbest ideas I've ever come up with. The shit isn't going to be good for my health. I didn't think this whole referring her for a job thing through, but I also had little choice in the matter.

Four years ago when Mia tore her ACL, a teammate told me during practice what happened and I almost hurled on the spot. I knew what an injury of that magnitude meant, and I knew that it would be the end of any sort of Olympic dream for Mia.

I remember that day like it was yesterday. I dropped everything to the ground and started running as fast as my legs would take me to my car. It was a second-hand Honda that my dad bought me my junior year of college, but it had just as much get up and go as I imagine it had the day it was built.

I practically flew on fumes to the hospital and when I arrived Mia was already heavily sedated and on her way to surgery. Because one of the nurses recognized who I was, she let me peek in on her before they took her to surgery.

"I'm here," I told her.

"Rush?"

"I'm here, Bird."

Tears cascaded down the sides of her face and into her ears.

"Finally, my good luck charm is here."

While I knew her words were said through the haze of anesthesia, they cut me to the bone.

I was her good luck charm.

She truly believed that.

And I let her down.

I've been trying to redeem myself ever since.

When I heard about this opening with the Hawks for a PT, I knew it was meant to be.

Another chance to redeem myself.

To be her hero.

Her lucky charm.

Sure, some of my motivation stems from guilt. My path to the NFL seemed to be laid out so easily for me, and Mia's journey has been a total ride on the struggle bus. We were both successful athletes in college, but now I'm the one with a 10,000 square foot house and a guaranteed multi-million dollar contract and she's worried about paying her rent in that shit apartment next month.

It isn't fair.

This isn't how it was supposed to be.

But all I can do is stay by her side, be her friend, and do however much she allows me to do for her.

For now anyway, that will have to be enough.

SEVENTEEN

RUSH

IT'S BEEN an average morning of training camp. I'm finally remembering all the rookies' names and memorizing the season's new plays, both of which have been hard tasks since I've been having trouble sleeping. Why? Because a little physical therapist I know has been haunting my dreams and making me wake in the middle of the night with a brick hard dick and no solution in sight.

That's why I've been ducking her at work.

It's a bitch move, but I feel like Mia would definitely see right through me if we spend any meaningful time in conversation. My eyes go straight for her tits and ass now. It's like I can't control the little fuckers. Eventually she's going to figure out that something is different with me and I'm not ready to have that conversation. Hell, I don't think she's ready to hear it. I almost went *there* the night she cooked me dinner, and she was practically running from me in her own damn house.

At first I thought, maybe I'll tell her. Maybe we could talk it through. Me dreaming that I'm banging the hell out of my best friend? Me wanting to actually act on some of those dreams? Then I came to my senses. That conversation would not go over well at all.

Mia has been working at her new job for three weeks now and she seems to have made a smooth adjustment into her role as a team physical therapist. The first week of her being a bright and shiny new object in the locker room has settled down now, and the guys are learning and accepting that she's a skilled clinician who is simply here to do a job.

Let me rephrase that.

Everyone is accepting that but Samuels.

Which is another reason why I can't sleep.

He thinks he's so slick, but I've been watching him out the corner of my eye at every turn. He's been sure not to cross any lines with Mia, but he's always there like a fly on shit. Smiling when she walks by on her way to a training room. Putting on a show for her when she's on the field and running fast like an Olympic sprinter. Conveniently eating when she's having lunch. Asking her questions about muscles he doesn't even know the names for.

I'm hip to his hustle.

He's slowly trying to groom her with his charming personality and humorous jokes, and once he thinks he's waited the appropriate amount of time, he's going to go in for the kill. Just because I asked him to back off, it feels as if he's going in even harder. He's fucking with me as if this is some sort of game to him, but he's going to learn very soon if he keeps it up, that I am not to be fucked with.

My mood improves once I notice Mia across the field. She's dressed in a pair of fitted black sweatpants with a thick stripe down the side and a white v-neck t-shirt with the Nighthawk logo. Even in the official team sweats, Bird looks sexy as fuck.

She hops into a golf cart and drives in my direction.

"You all right?" I ask her, doing my best to keep my eyes on hers and not on how good her tits look in that white shirt.

"Are you going to ask me that every time I see you? It's been a month, *paw-paw*."

"It's been three weeks."

Three weeks and she still isn't using her cane.

"Where's your cane?"

"I don't need it today."

"You sure you aren't pushing yourself too hard, Bird?"

"I'm sure. It's like the spirits know I need to be on my A game and are looking out for me. I haven't had any serious pain in weeks. She lifts both her knees with her hands on her hips to show me how limber she is.

"Remember when I used to dance all the time, Rush?"

"I remember."

"I was a force of nature."

"You can still dance."

"Not like then," she recalls wistfully. "Now I'm just happy to show you I can bend and lift my knees."

My eyes drop to the ground. It saddens me that she's not able to be that free spirited girl around the bonfire. I wish she would let me find her a surgeon and pay for it. It's literally killing me that a possible fix is out there and it's beyond her grasp because of money. Money I have.

"Do you want to get dinner with me on your break today?" she asks.

I notice Samuels staring at the two of us clear across the field. It's like a chess match. He's waiting to see which one of my pieces I'm going to play. Unfortunately, I'm out of moves today.

"Me and Carter, the one who jabbed me in the face during the melee in the locker room, have actually hit it off. I promised him that I'd help run a drill during break."

"Your dinner break is for dinner. When are you going to eat?"

"I was going to wait and eat a big meal after camp. I've been snacking on stuff all day."

Mia pouts and crosses her arms in front of her, lifting her breasts up front and center. Does she know her nipples are poking through that shirt? Fuck, if I see them then everyone sees them.

"We see each other every day but we have spent no time together. If I didn't think it was such a crazy assumption, I'd say that you were avoiding me, Rush Bacchetti."

Didn't I tell you?

She calls me on my shit every single time.

"I'm just busy trying to get ready for the season. I told you it would be busy like this during camp."

"All I'm asking for is dinner."

Of course I'm not going to tell her no.

I never can.

"Okay, Mia. Grab some food for us from the cafeteria and meet me here at five. I'll eat with you and work with Carter at the same time."

"Perfect," she happily sing-songs. "See you at five."

****

"What are you laughing at, Proctor?"

Our star running back has been eavesdropping on the sideline.

"Sorry, man, I don't mean to laugh but I've never seen you act like this in all the time I've known you."

"Act like what?"

"I'm starting to think that Mia is more to you than just a

college friend, and what was that name you were calling her? Was it bird?"

I lower my eyes from the truth of his comment. I'm sick of not telling people who Mia is and what she means to me. It was stupid of me to even hide it from the beginning. Anyone with half of a brain can see that I can't keep my eyes off of her.

"I'll admit she isn't just someone I knew from school."

"I knew it!" He exclaims.

"Don't get it twisted," I tell him. "Mia is my best friend and has been for years."

Proctor's face crinkles in confusion.

"Your best friend?"

"Yeah."

"Why is that a secret?"

"I didn't want the team to think I pulled some sort of special favor to get her the job." Which I kind of did.

"I get it. You didn't want the guys questioning her skills as a therapist."

"Exactly."

Finally, someone who gets it.

Proctor glares at me strangely, though.

"What?" I say to him.

"Does she know?"

"Know what?"

"That your feelings for her have changed."

"I don't know what you're talking about, Proctor."

"Or maybe they've always been there all along, simmering quietly in the friend zone. Because if I see it, you best believe some other people are going to notice. The only one who may not realize it is the one person who should."

"You're way off base. She's like my sister."

"I actually have a sister and trust me when I tell you

that I've never stared at her tits and ass the way you watch Mia's."

I want to shut him the fuck up. His words are only making the slow realization I've been coming to about Mia feel even more real. I've always told myself that I sometimes look at her body because she's a beautiful woman and I'm only human, but now I'm thinking differently. I guess Proctor is right. If she was "really" my sister, I wouldn't look at her in that way. In fact, I'd need to go on a therapist's couch if I did.

"I need to go watch tape in the video room." I'm ending this conversation. "I'll get up with you later."

He chuckles to himself then asks me the last question I need to hear.

"What are you going to do about that fucker Samuels?"

"What about him? I thought he was your problem."

"You better watch him. I wasn't lying about my mother. He slept with her and now he's pursuing Mia hard. He's got a way with the ladies that is almost pimp-like. "

"Not my lady," I counter.

"Ohhhh, okay," he smiles. "So she's your lady now?"

"You know what I mean."

"I know exactly what you mean. Just make sure that she does too before it's too late."

I'm annoyed.

I don't enjoy talking about my personal business with anyone, but Proctor brings up a valid point. What am I going to do about Samuels? I'll break his fucking jaw if he puts a hand on Mia, but if Mia allows Samuels to get close to her, and dare I say becomes interested in him, how am I going to stop it?

How am I going to stop him?

EIGHTEEN

MIA

ONE PERK of being on the Nighthawk training campus is that they have one of the coolest cafeterias I've ever seen, if that's what you want to call it. It's a massive area that acts as the heart of the facility for players and staff. There's a sitting area that can accommodate up to a hundred and fifty people, flat-screen TVs hanging on the walls and every corner, and an outdoor stone patio complete with a fireplace and brick oven.

The dining hall looks more like an upscale hotel restaurant than a cafeteria, and it's run like a tight ship by a petite woman with chestnut brown skin and a short blonde pixie cut (Jada Pinkett styled) who is the team's official dietician.

All I have to do is make a selection and request dinner for two to take on the field and they conveniently package up two scrumptious looking Mediterranean meals of grilled chicken and shrimp skewers, roasted veggies and hummus and pita bread on the side. It's like I've died and gone to food porn heaven. All healthy meals and snacks that are scrumptious and made fresh every single day. What more could a girl ask for?

While I'm waiting for them to package everything up nicely, Tiger Samuels approaches me at the counter.

"Hey, Mia."

My face brightens once I see it's him. Samuels has been one of the nicest players I've met on the team so far and is always a lot of fun to chat with.

"Hi, Samuels. What's up with you?"

"Mia, you should really call me Tiger."

"Doesn't everyone call you by your last name? I thought that was the protocol around here."

"Tiger is the name my Mama gave me and I'd like it if one person in this building would use it."

"Understood." I smile. "Tiger it is."

"So where are you sitting for dinner?" he asks.

"Oh, I'm going to take it to down to the field."

"You're working with someone through break?"

"Well, no, I'm going to eat with Rush. Just to catch up on things."

"Oh, I see."

Samuels (I mean Tiger) seems disappointed and I feel a little bad about it. From what I can tell, he and Rush are friendly and he's been so welcoming toward me, I'd hate for him to feel as if I'm excluding him. It's not like I'm going to have Rush's full attention, anyway. He's going to be working with Carter.

"Feel free to join us," I offer. "Rush is working with Carter while we eat."

His facial expression shifts immediately.

"I'd love to. What did you order?"

"I got the Mediterranean dinner. Chicken and shrimp skewers. They look fantastic."

"I'll get an order of that too," he tells the one of the cafeteria staff. "With extra pita and hummus."

"Sure thing, Samuels," the worker says.

"I love pita and hummus too," I tell him.

"Great minds think alike," he quips. "We'll share."

As we exit the common area with our dinner, I'm surprised to find that Rush is waiting in front of the building in the driver's seat of a golf cart. His mouth turns downwards into a deep scowl once he sees me exiting the dining commons with Tiger, although I'm not exactly sure why. I thought they were friends.

"Oh great, Rush is here with our ride," Tiger says facetiously as he grabs the bags out of my hand and offers the crook of his arm to help me inside the cart.

I don't need his help, but I feel weird leaving him hanging, so I grab it and slide into the hard white backseat of the cart.

"Why are you here?" Rush asks Tiger, and it's the rudest I've seen him act in a long time.

"Having dinner with you and Mia. It's Mediterranean tonight, and I was invited to tag along."

He looks for me out of the corner of his eyes.

"We've got extra pita and hummus," I say awkwardly.

"Fine, get in," he growls.

Rush presses on the accelerator so fast that both Tiger and I go jerking backwards.

"Hey!" I protest, but Rush doesn't even apologize. He just silently drives us over to the area where he's working with Carter.

There are various tables set up on the sides of the field close to the bleachers and I happily unpack and spread the food on one of them sort of buffet style. The canteen gave us so much food that even if Carter wants to nosh, there's enough for all of us.

Rush is still acting like a total dick and is giving Tiger an icy glare as he chews ravenously on a skewer of chicken. I guess he's only eating chicken and shrimp today. He never eats out-of-order like this. Normally he would have had the roasted veggies first.

"So what was Rush like in school?" Tiger asks, trying to make conversation.

I eat a forkful of my perfectly seasoned roasted vegetables before I answer.

"Very much like he is now." I look at Rush. "Quiet, talented, and a great friend."

"And what were you like?" he asks.

"Loud, talented and the best friend a man could have," Rush answers before I can respond.

"*Best* friends?" Tiger questions incredulously.

"The best," Rush retorts yet again.

Rush watches for my reaction after he's said the words, but I'm okay. The semi-charade we've been up to is over, which is fine with me. I think that everyone on the team is viewing me as a valuable therapist now. They've seen what I can do.

"Oh, I didn't realize."

"Well, you wouldn't," Rush counters. "You've known her for what, two seconds?"

"Rush." I admonish him. "You're being really grouchy today."

"I'm fine, Mia."

Carter jogs over and disrupts the reckoning I was almost ready to give Rush.

"Ready, Rush?" He asks eagerly.

Rush looks hesitantly between me and Tiger, grabs a shrimp skewer, and then responds to his new protege.

"Let's go, Carter. We're working on speed today. You'll start with twenty-five sprints."

"Got you."

Carter and Rush head further out onto the practice field to work on his sprints as Tiger and I sit and get to know one each other a little better.

"Stay on the balls of your feet!" Rush shouts over to Carter. "Swing your arms from eye to hip. Not across your body."

"Do you think Rush is annoyed that I've interrupted your dinner with him?" Tiger asks.

"Absolutely not. He's just a crabby patty by nature."

"Mia, can you bring me another skewer?" Rush interrupts.

"Are your hands broken?" I taunt him like we always do with each other. Now that the true nature of our friendship has been revealed to at least one person, I feel as if we can start to finally be normal with each other.

Tiger laughs at my little jibe, but Rush doesn't. He turns around and stares menacingly at the two of us.

"I'm working." He turns back to Carter. "Keep your chest up and drive your knees up seventy-five to ninety degrees."

"It's dinner break," I bite back. "Come over here and eat your food yourself."

"Wow," Tiger remarks. "I'm not used to hearing people talk to the infamous Rush Bacchetti like this. It's refreshing."

When Rush glares angrily at me, I realize that I may have just inserted my size nine foot into my feisty little mouth. Without another word between us, I grab both a shrimp and chicken skewer off the table and walk it over to him. He notices that I'm walking slower than usual and his face drops. Before he can apologize, Tiger jogs over and wraps his arm around my waist to support my weight.

"You ok there, Mia?"

"Yes," I answer gently. "Just making sure my friend here eats since he's *working*."

I can tell that Rush is still upset, but I'm not exactly sure if it's with me or himself.

"Samuels, can you grab a pair of crutches for Mia in the PT main office? Anybody in there will know where they are."

"I should have thought of that myself. Let me go grab you a pair, Mia."

After Tiger jogs off toward the center, Rush grabs the two skewers out of my hand and polishes each one off as I stand in front of him with my mouth agape.

NINETEEN

MIA

"Why did you ask him to do that?"

"You need them."

"Are you determined to make me look weak in front of everyone on this team? First, you help me get this job and now you're purposely sabotaging me?"

The pupils of his eyes darken.

"You're upset so I'm going to pretend you didn't say that shit."

"You jackass–"

He lifts his hand to stop me from saying anything more.

"The crutches say your pain is temporary to people, but the cane might communicate something else more permanent. So I'm thinking that the compromise here is to use the crutches when you need them at work and use your cane at home."

"I don't need to make any compromises with you."

"I'm not going to be able to come to work every day and watch you make stupid decisions when you're clearly in pain, Mia. I won't fucking do it."

"Is it possible for us to *not* talk about my leg for one

day?" I'm so irritated with him I could scream. If I didn't need this job so badly, I would quit. "Are you my friend or my freakin' doctor?"

The player Rush has been running drills with notices that we're having words and stops sprinting to see if we're both okay.

"You okay, Rush?"

Correction, he's just checking on the superstar he clearly idolizes.

"Fine," Rush confirms. "Work on the left foot's lift off. It's slower than the right."

"Okay."

I'm fine thanks for asking.

"Mia, I'm just looking out for you."

"I don't need you to look out for me. Some days my knee hurts and some days it doesn't. I'm a physical therapist. I know what I'm doing."

Tiger is across the field talking to another player. He's standing with a pair of crutches in his hand, which he foraged for me from somewhere in the training center in record time. He lifts one in the air to show me he has them, and I wave back and smile.

At the same time, a stray football comes flying in our direction from mid field and before either of us can react the ball hits Rush in exactly the same place he was injured a few weeks ago.

"Fuck!"

His hand immediately holds the side of his face and I do my best to hold in a laugh, but it's no use. The guffaw explodes from deep inside of my belly. The back-up quarterback who threw the ball calls out an apology to Rush.

"Are you ok?" I ask through tears of laughter streaming down my face.

"I see that my pain has moved you to tears."

"I'm sorry," I say as I try to settle myself down. "It's just that you're so worried about what's going on with me you didn't notice that there was a ball headed straight for you. I mean, you literally had to be bonked on the head to be reminded to mind your own damn business. If that's not a sign, I don't know what is."

I hold my hand over my mouth after that to stop any runaway giggles. Then Rush does the most beautiful thing. He laughs too. It's a deep, boisterous sound that comes deep from within his gut and one of my most favorite sounds in the world.

He picks up the stray ball and throws it back midfield, then walks closer to me and places a hand on my shoulder. I internally stiffen from the contact, not because I mind it, but because it's unexpected. We're outside and exposed for anyone to see, and I'm usually the touchy-feely one in our friendship, not Rush.

"I'm sorry, Bird."

"Me too."

"I don't want you to think that I don't want you here. I do. It's just going to take a little more getting used to than I thought."

"Okay."

Rush runs his hand through his hair in what I know is a tactic to silence himself, so he says nothing more. It's a bad habit. He should express himself more, but we're all works in progress—even someone as wonderful as Rush.

"Friends argue," I assure him. "Let's forget about it."

He checks the time on his sports watch.

"We have little time left for dinner break, but how about we hang for a little while at my place tonight."

"Okay."

"What do you want to do? A movie?"

"Let's do yoga tonight!"

I've been influential in getting Rush to take up yoga for the last few years. It helps athletes so much with their flexibility and strength, and Rush will try almost anything that will give him an edge over his opponents.

"Cool, we haven't done that together in a while."

Once Tiger approaches, he hands me my new crutches and watches both of us with a curious look.

"Here you go, Mia."

"Thank you so much."

The crutches are a little short for me, but I'll make an adjustment once I get back to the training center.

"Is your leg going to be okay? When did you hurt it?"

I look at Rush, then back to Tiger.

"It's an old college injury that sometimes acts up."

"You were an athlete?"

"I was a volleyball player."

"I can totally see that. I bet you were good."

"She was great," Rush gushes.

"Now I understand how you and our boy here met," Tiger says. He seems to be pleased with this recent information about us. "So, Mia, I'm going to this fundraising thing in two weeks and was wondering if you might want to come with me?"

"What kind of fundraiser?"

"I'm an ambassador for an organization that's dedicated to eradicating child hunger in New York City. They're hosting a celebrity softball game at Yankee Stadium. It's pretty low key. I'd do an early morning here and then go there in the afternoon."

"And you want me to go?"

"I don't like to go to those things alone. It would be nice to have a friend along."

"Is this a date?" I joke.

Tiger looks at Rush whose mouth is in a tight, straight line and then back at me.

"We don't have to put a name on it. Just thought we could hang."

"Sure, I'd love to. Let's exchange information."

After about fifteen minutes, Rush has said little of anything to either of us as we finish the rest of our dinner. He's been watching Carter run his sprints with a careful eye, shoveling hummus in his mouth, completely eating his dinner out of food group order.

When he finally speaks again, it's to only say five words to me and then he takes off jogging cross field.

"I'll see you tonight, Bird."

TWENTY

MIA

EVERY SINGLE TIME I pull up to Rush's impressive circular stone driveway, I'm always in awe, as if it's the first time I'm visiting. I feel as if I'm on a tour of Hollywood's celebrity homes. There are carefully manicured bushes and ornamental shrubs which flank the front of the property, and his doorbell has the longest chime I'm ever heard, with seven specific bell tones that take forever to finish ringing. It's definitely a house that says *I've arrived*, but it still makes me wonder, why would a single man live in an enormous mansion like this that stays empty half of the year?

Rush answers the door shirtless, in basketball shorts, with a layer of sweat all over his face. I work with half-naked athletes every day, but there's a part of me that makes me want to avert my eyes because there's something about seeing Rush half-clothed that feels intimate and private, or else I'm just hopelessly horny.

"Hey."

"Uh, hey yourself. You remembered I was coming tonight, right?"

"I was just working on some core exercises before you got here."

"Are you going to shower?"

"Who showers before yoga, Mia? Just come inside."

"That doorbell of yours is something. When did you get that?"

"I don't know, maybe like six months ago."

He grabs my messenger bag and the pink yoga mat out of my hand and leads me to one of the many unused rooms on the first floor of the house.

"We'll do yoga in here. I even set the temperature of the room to ninety degrees so it feels more like hot yoga."

"You can alter the temperature of one room in the house? I've never heard of that."

"It's called a zone heating system. I had it put in because it's energy efficient, and I don't have to heat the entire house at the same temperature. If I want, I can just make it warmer in certain rooms, like my bedroom, during the winter months. Same thing with the air conditioning in the summer."

"Look at you being all energy conscious. I must be rubbing off on you."

"A little."

He licks the corner of his mouth in the most sexy way.

Oh God, I must be PMSing.

"The heat is supposed to be good for the soreness in your knee, right?" He asks. "Oh wait, forget I said anything. We're not supposed to be talking about your knee anymore. I'm done with that."

"You're making progress, Bacchetti." I grin. "Tonight is just about two friends having a hot yoga session and maybe some popcorn afterwards. No, take care of Mia chit-chat. It's a habit I'm determined to break you out of."

After several minutes of warm-ups and our usual yoga routine that we have done before, Rush decides he wants to try a few new moves that including him lifting me. He even has examples of the poses on his phone for a visual reference.

"I'm going to lift you up like this," he shows me. "It'll help increase my core strength."

We've never tried couple yoga poses before, but I hesitantly agree.

"Okay, but first let's wipe down. All this sweat is gross."

"That's the point of hot yoga."

"If you want to lift me, you'll wipe down."

"Fine," he chuckles.

Rush takes a clean white towel that's folded in the room's corner and wipes himself down. The innocent act seems down right salacious to watch. Each of his sculpted muscles ripple as he dries himself off from head to toe. Then he grabs another towel, but instead of handing it to me, he gently wipes me down next. He starts with my forehead and my nose, then methodically wipes the sweat, dabs the sweat away from my arms, chest, stomach and legs.

Holy shit, that was erotic.

"Ready?" He asks in his rich, baritone voice.

"Uh, huh?"

Rush lies on his back with his knees to his chest.

"Lay your hips on my feet," he instructs. "Just like the picture."

I position my hips while his hands anchor my shoulders. Then he extends both of his legs and arms and lifts me face down into the air. I'm impressed that we are actually pulling off an intermediate pose like this. I make sure to extend my entire body stiff as a board as he holds me steady as if I'm light as a feather.

The two of us remain focused and determined to maintain the hold while looking into each other's eyes or more aptly put into each other's souls. It's the most vulnerable I think we've ever been with each other.

"You want to try another?" he asks in a deep, raspy voice.

"Sure."

This time we try an even more challenging pose. He shows me the example and I cringe a little.

"I don't know, Rush, this one looks hard."

"It'll either work or it won't but we won't know unless we try."

"Right, okay."

I start curled on top of his body with his hands on my shoulders and his legs in a ninety-degree angle.

"Push off and forward with your feet."

Once I push myself forward, Rush straightens his arms and pushes up my shoulders until my entire body is straight in the air with my hands holding his ankles for support and his hands keeping me steady and in the air.

This one is definitely hard.

"Point your toes," he orders.

I waver for a moment, but he holds me steady. The anchor in this pose needs to have amazing core and arm strength to pull it off and Rush is amazing on both of those fronts.

We breathe deeply and hold the pose for a few seconds more, and then he gently lowers me down until I am lying completely on top of him. I lie on top of him for just a moment longer than I probably should, but it just feels so good.

I love physical touch. I got little it from my mom growing up, so I think that's why I look for it so desperately from other people. I like it best though when it comes from Rush.

"This kind of reminds me of the workouts we used to do at the beach back in Miami," Rush says, and the delicious rumble of his words vibrates through his chest into mine.

My body sinks even further into his.

"Those were the good ole' days," I respond. "We didn't know how lucky we were to have a school so close to the beach. A lot of us took it for granted."

"You and those bonfires."

"And all that drinking we did."

"You definitely did."

"Yeah, I was a bit of a lush in college. That's because my Grandma was so strict with me in high school. I didn't have my first drink until freshman week in Miami."

"Not one drink in high school? Not even a cooler or a beer?"

"Not one drop."

"I drank little in college, but I definitely experimented a little in high school. Back then we all thought we were so grown."

"I'm sure that wasn't much of an experiment."

"A few beers now and then."

"You have always been so dedicated to your clean diet and smart decisions and look at everything you have to show for it. I'm so proud of you, Rush. You've achieved everything you set out to do on those handmade vision boards we created our freshman year of college. You've got the career, the accolades, the big house, the fancy car, and you take care of your parents too. You have everything."

"I don't have *everything* I want, Bird."

"Well, then, you're a greedy boy," I jest, patting his chest with my hand.

I don't want to move from this spot but I have to or I'm going to sweat all over his body and not in the *good-and-freaky way* but rather in a *yuck-we-need-a-shower-right-now-way*. It's getting hot as hell in this room.

"Is there any water in here?" I ask.

"I'll get it."

Rush grabs us a couple of bottled waters and we sit back down cross-legged on our mats.

"Whatever happened to that girl from California? The pretty one from the School Of Business who you really liked senior year?"

"She was insecure."

"I wouldn't have pegged her for the insecure type."

"She thought you and I were a little too close. She wanted me to stop spending so much time with you. She said it made her look stupid."

"You never told me that."

"Eh, it didn't matter that much to me so I moved on."

I silently nod in understanding. Our friendship has made romantic relationships with other people complicated for us many times over the years, but none of those people were worth abandoning each other for. If our partners weren't strong enough to accept our friendship, then they weren't the right partners for us. At least that's the way I always looked at it.

"I'm going to use the bathroom before we do our cool down."

"You know where it is. Down the hall to the left."

"Yep."

I'm comfortable walking with bare feet to Rush's first floor bathroom. His house is immaculate and his powder room has a pristine and spa-like quality to it. The entire bathroom is covered in cream marble tile with these taupe colored veins running through the stone. There's a modern square sink with a shiny chrome waterfall type faucet and a toilet with a self-warming toilet seat. Even the disposable hand towels are fancy, each embossed with a gold B in the center. I don't even want to use one to dry my hands because they're so pretty.

It's been a while since I've been inside of Rush's house, but it's clear that someone has added designer touches to the interior since I've been here last. Rush would have never thought to add things with this much detail in his guest powder room. It's seriously making me wonder whether he's sleeping with an interior decorator or a freakin' host from HGTV.

After I reluctantly use one of the hand towels to dry my freshly washed hands, I exit to find Rush sitting at the bottom of his front staircase holding his bowed head in between his hands.

"Bacchetti, when did you hire a decorator? Your bathroom looks like something I've seen on an episode of Gossip Girl. I love it!"

But Rush doesn't move an inch or make a sound.

And a feeling of dread envelops me.

Something is very wrong.

TWENTY-ONE

MIA

"An email alert came in on your phone," Rush says in a deadly calm voice.

He's wiggles my cell phone in his hand like it's a smoking gun.

"It lit up like a Christmas tree, so it was hard to ignore."

"Okay, *soooo?*" I say.

"Why didn't you tell me what was going on with your building, Mia?"

Shit. Shit. Double shit.

"I'm handling it, Rush. I didn't tell you because I knew you'd react like this."

"I'm reacting like this because you're not handling it!" he explodes. "You are on a month-to-month lease and they are choosing not to renew it because of back rent. And by the date of the first email in this string, it looks like you've known about this for quite some time."

"That's just their way of getting out of bringing the building up to code. I made a complaint about the elevators and the fact that there is no handicapped entrance into the building and now they want to evict me. I don't need the ramp, but what if I did? What about people who are in wheelchairs or use walkers?"

"The owner is completely within his or her rights not to renew your lease if you don't pay the rent on time."

"But they're breaking the law by not having the elevators working."

"I was just there, and they were working fine."

"They work for a week or two and then a part breaks and they're offline for another few weeks. It happens all the time."

"You never told me that shit."

"I don't tell you everything, Rush."

"Well, maybe you should start telling me everything. What do you do when the elevators aren't working?"

"Obviously, I walk up the stairs."

"You walk up five flights of stairs with that knee?"

"Yes."

He stands up and takes several heavy strides toward me, then stops.

For a split second, I'm frightened, but not because I think Rush would ever lay his hands on me, but because he's so emotional about this. About my life. He really cares about me in a way that no one ever has. Even my own mother.

It almost feels like love.

"Rush."

I place my palm on his chest and feel nothing but solid muscle and warm skin that shivers underneath my touch.

His eyes hold mine perfectly still.

"Why won't you let me help you, Bird?"

His voice croaks when he speaks, and he sounds like he is in actual physical pain. It's frightening to me that I have the power to make him feel this upset.

I lift myself on my toes and kiss him softly on the cheek because something inside of me compels me to. In response, he leans his body into mine and kisses me gingerly on the lips, then stares at me with fiery eyes that want more from me in this moment than I can give.

"I'm going to sue them, Rush."

"With what money?" he responds in a much calmer voice now.

"Maybe someone will take the case pro bono. It's totally winnable. Landlords shouldn't treat people like this."

I try to move back and give us both some space, but he won't let me. He wraps one of his arms loosely around my waist and holds me still in front of him.

"Are we friends?"

"Of course we are."

"Then can you tell me the truth for once? The whole truth."

"I admit I haven't always told you everything, but when I do tell you something I always tell you the truth. I've never lied to you and I never will."

"Then answer this question. Are you late on all of your bills right now? Are you in trouble, Mia?"

I consider what exact words I'm going to use to answer this in a way that Rush will understand. Once upon a time we were both college students on full-ride scholarships to a prestigious university. We've grown up together, sharing a lot of personal highs and lows with each other. Now we're like two completely different people who tragically don't live in the same world any longer. I don't want to be the girl in his life that he has to fix.

The friend he pities.

The dead weight.

The woman he has to save over and over.

I cannot be that girl.

"I'm late on everything but definitely catching up. I was paid my first paycheck a week ago. Things are getting better."

"I have a proposition for you, Bird, and it's not because of what I've just learned today but it's something I've been thinking about for a long time."

"What is it?"

"I'm away for half of the season playing games in other cities, and I pay a service to manage this house. They make sure that the utilities are paid and that the landscapers and cleaning service comes once a week to do their jobs. They even make sure the fridge is stocked with my favorite foods a day or two before I'm due to arrive home and that someone comes in to feed the fish. They make sure that this place runs like a well-oiled machine, and I pay them a lot of money to keep it that way."

"I don't get where you're going with this."

"I think you should do it instead and you live here while you do it. Keep an eye on the place and run the house for me."

"I realize you were hit in the face with a football today, but I think it knocked all the common sense out of you. Are you crazy?"

"What's crazy about it?" he asks with a dead serious look on his face.

"I have a job."

"I wouldn't pay you. It would be a barter situation. Room and board in exchange for your services."

"I don't need a house. I have a place to live."

He holds the phone up high again.

"Clearly not for much longer, and even if I paid the rent

for you, I don't want you living in a building where the elevators work fifty percent of the time."

"Rush, this is insane."

"If we had been regular college students, and I didn't go play with the Nighthawks straight out of school, it could have been a real possibility that we would have been roommates, anyway."

"But that's not our reality."

"Let's be real about this. It's either that we go with my brilliant idea or I give you a loan to move out of the apartment, move into a new place, and catch up on all of your bills. And let me tell you what I know for sure. I know how high rentals in this area can be because of our close proximity to New York City. I know you don't make enough money to pay your current bills and catch up on the old ones. I know you send Mandy money every month to pay her bills. I know that what I'm proposing could give you a minute to catch your fucking breath, and then I could stop worrying about your ass all the damn time."

"I'm not your responsibility. I never told you to worry."

"You sound incredibly naïve and selfish right now. Of course I worry. You think it's easy for me to have so much money at my disposal, and the person I most care about in this world won't let me use it to help her?"

I'm the person he cares about *most* in this world? While I'm happy to hear him say the words, the significance of that statement weighs heavily on my heart. I need to do the right thing here for the both of us because I'm afraid that making a mistake would crush us both.

My feelings for Rush are changing while his are sure and steady. I'm attracted to him in a way that I thought I'd never be. In a way, that's very dangerous. The whole time we were practicing yoga today, I prayed that his hand didn't slip anywhere between my legs because then he'd know. He'd know that my body is betraying me in the rudest way possible.

Nipples hard.

Clit pulsing.

Panties wet.

I'm doing my best to keep my urges at bay because I refuse to sabotage our friendship. It's literally the only relationship I can depend on. So, no, this plan of his doesn't sound like a good idea.

I'm not going to lose the only friend I've got in this world.

No matter what.

"Our lives are already entangled because of work, but we've barely told anyone there that we're friends. How will we tell them we're roommates?"

"We don't have to tell them anything that you don't want to tell them. We have different schedules, two cars, and our own lives. Your paycheck is direct deposited, not sent in the mail. No one has to know, especially because it would be a temporary situation, and frankly because it's nobody's business."

I'm starting to waver.

It's a plan so nuts that it almost makes complete sense. We're friends who trust each other and enjoy each other's company. It wouldn't be like I was taking a handout. I'd be running his house, which is something I can do with my eyes closed and my hands tied behind my back. In high school, I was the one who took care of the house bills because my mother was too angry at the world to take care of them herself. I could definitely do this. I'd just have to be careful with his heart... and mine.

Suddenly a weight feels like it's being lifted off of my

chest. I wouldn't have to pay rent or utilities or worry about whether the elevator was working on any given day. I could catch up on my car note payments and save Grandma's house. I could use the money I bank away to finally schedule the third and final surgery I need to become whole again. And I wouldn't have to sing myself to death to feel lighter. In fact, my spirit actually feels more buoyant in this moment than it has in a really long time.

"This will be weird," I tell him. "Our dynamic would be different."

"Nothing has to be weird about it if we don't let it. You're still my best friend, Bird. Nothing more and nothing less. I just want you to be okay."

Nothing more and nothing less. Not exactly the sentiment my heart wanted to hear, but exactly the words my head needed to hear. This is an arrangement between friends that will be beneficial for both of us. *A platonic arrangement, Mia.* I can do this because I think Rush needs this just as much as I do. It's just in his nature to want to see me safe, and I have to learn how to start respecting that if we're going to remain friends.

I wrap my arms around his waist and squeeze hard.

Good gravy, even sweaty he smells yummy.

"That's the nicest thing that anyone has every said to me. They broke the mold when they made you, Bacchetti."

"And my offer?"

"When do I move in?"

RUSH

THE LAST ASSIGNMENT for my house management team was to arrange for Mia's move. It took some persuasion, but she finally permitted me to have a moving company come and help her pack most of her things.

"They can pack up everything but my panty drawer, my crystals, and my vibrator collection. That would just be nasty."

I almost spit a mouth full of cranberry juice clear across the room when she announced that. A vibrator collection? My dick gets instantaneously hard thinking about Mia in bed, legs spread wide, and using one of those on herself. Who the fuck is she thinking about when she slides it inside? I shiver at the thought.

"Not a problem, Bird." I pretend as if I'm unfazed. "Just tell them what to do and they'll follow your directions."

The moving company packs her up in record time and leaves the apartment cleaner than when she probably moved in. I know she won't get her security deposit back because of the back rent, but I don't want them fining her for any cleaning issues either. Landlords are notorious for that shit, and I just want that chapter of her life closed.

My plan for the night Mia came over for yoga last week was to talk to her about Samuels and finally tell her what he's been accused of doing with Proctor's mother. After that shit he pulled at camp, asking her for a date to a charity event he doesn't give two shits about, I thought it was time she learned the truth about him. He's not just some personable, cuddly football player who gets way more press than he deserves. He's a user and someone with very little respect for women. But since she's moved into my house, and we spend most of our free time together, I think Samuels is a non-issue now. She may not be in my bed, but she is intertwined in my life in all the other ways that matter. There's no need for me to rock the boat and push her for anything more than what she has always given me, her unwavering support and friendship. I can get ass from any woman, but that right there..is priceless.

Having the move behind us, I think I can safely say that this has been the greatest idea I've ever had (if I say so myself). Mia has a roof over her head, I finally got a good night's sleep for the first time in weeks, and because she's in my house, I can keep an eye on her and that knee. Phase two of this arrangement is finding a way to pay for Mia's surgery and make her think it was all her idea.

I give Bird the second largest bedroom in the house. I've never used the room for much and it's decorated with natural earth tones, which is actually going to be great because it's like a blank pallet for Mia to add her own unique and colorful touches.

"I thought you'd like the windows," I explain as she twirls slowly around in the middle of the room. Today is a good day for her knee.

"This room is bigger than my entire apartment."

"You've seen this room a thousand times, Bird." I downplay it.

"I never paid that much attention to it before, but now that it's mine, it seems that much more impressive."

"I gave you the room with the arched windows facing East because I knew you'd like the morning light for your plants."

"Mork and Mindy will love it in here."

"Who the hell gives their plants names?"

"I do."

"Ridiculous."

"If you were a plant, wouldn't you want your mama to give you a name?"

"I never considered it."

"Your fish have names."

I had a large aquarium filled with freshwater sharks installed downstairs about six months ago when I made some other updates to my house. I got it because the aquarium looks cool in my den, not because I really acknowledge them as pets.

"The fish don't have names."

"You better be kidding me, Rush Bacchetti."

"They're decoration."

"They're pets!"

"I tell you what, Bird, you can name them for me."

"Someone should name them. This is tantamount to abuse."

"Oh, settle down. Add it to your list of house management duties."

"We've got another problem."

"What?"

"Where am I going to put my sofa?"

"In the trash?"

"Not funny."

"I'll move it in here. There's plenty of space for it."

"A sofa in my room?"

"People do it all the time."

"People like the Queen of England?

"Lots of people decorate their bedrooms with sofas who aren't royalty, Mia. Maybe it's a southern thing, but my parents had a small sofa in their room my entire life. The idea is that you don't have to sit on your bed in your street clothes."

"Oh, I guess that makes sense. Then I'll put it over there." She points. "It'll be a nice pop of color against all of this beige."

"We can paint the room if you want."

"Absolutely not. I can jazz things up in here without going through all of that."

I'm sure she can.

"I've got a surprise for you," I tell her.

"I'm scared to ask. You've done so much already."

"I've hard-wired the house with a speaker system and connected them to Wi-Fi. All you have to do is tell a speaker anywhere in the house what song you want to hear and he'll play it all over the house."

"He?"

"He's like Alexa or Siri except that I named him Michael and I gave him an Irish accent."

Michael Jackson is Mia's favorite artist, and lately she has a thing for people with Irish accents. So there you have it. A perfect hybrid.

She spots the small speaker in the upper corner of her bedroom.

"Michael, play man in the mirror."

A voice that sounds like Irish actor, Colin Farrell, responds and Bird's' face lights up like a Friday night in Times Square.

God, I love it when she looks like that.

Playing *Man In The Mirror*, by Michael Jackson

My home becomes transformed as inspirational words (of my least favorite Michael Jackson song) practically bounce off the walls of every room in the house. Mia raises her arms high, snapping her fingers and swinging her hips as she sings along or rather on top of the vocals. As usual, she's off-key, loud, vibrant, infectious and joy bounces off of her like gamma rays.

That's when phase three of this arrangement hits me like a lightening bolt.

If I want *this* in my life, always.

If I don't want this amazing woman to ever leave this house.

I'm going to have to make her fall in love with me.

MIA

Iт's hot as a frying pan today and the air conditioning in the green goblin is on the fritz, but none of that matters to me because all is right with the world. Work is not work at all, it's fun; and the last few weeks at Rush's house have been a much needed respite. I get to see one of my favorite people in the world every day at work and at home; I was able to send my mother the rest of the money she needed for the real estate taxes, and my appointment with the new ortho surgeon is next week.

I finally had to have a truthful conversation with Scott about the nature of my injury and he was more than willing to give me a day off for the consultation. In fact, he pretty much volunteered to be the therapist who builds a treatment plan for me after the surgery, which I can probably schedule at some point during the offseason. I thought it was really cool of him to offer.

Today I have Tiger, Darius and Rush in my therapy rotation. I'm working on some back exercises with Tiger, more hamstring exercises with Darius, and finally some preventative neck and shoulder stretching for Rush.

"The weirdest thing happened today in my therapy meeting," I tell Rush in a hushed voice.

"What?"

"We were working on next week's schedule and Scott mentioned we will no longer schedule Tiger and Proctor at the same time until further notice."

"Did he say why?"

"No, I thought you'd know. I mean you all have to practice together, so why would we have to alter our therapy schedules around for them?"

"I don't gossip about my teammates."

"Dude, it's not gossip. It's a legitimate question."

"A question that you should have asked your boss."

"Just by your reaction, I know there's some juicy gossip behind the decision."

I'm standing behind Rush, who's seated on a chair. I am slowly rotating his head three-hundred-and-sixty degrees to gently stretch his neck. He's had a little neck pain in the past from sudden movements or collisions on the field, so it's something that the strength and PT teams monitor.

"How's that feel?" I ask.

"Good."

I notice a tiny tattoo on his neck that I haven't seen before because it's surrounded by so many others. I glide my finger over the ink. It's a small parakeet with wings so intricate only a master artist could have done it.

"When did you get this?"

"Last time I was in Los Angeles."

"That's where your regular tattoo artist is, right?"

"Yeah."

"It's a parakeet."

"I know what it is."

"Why'd you get that?"

"They're small birds with large personalities."

"Like me?" I ask, slightly panicked.

It's not that I have a problem with it, it's just that I'm astonished by the sentiment if the tattoo was actually intended to represent me.

"Don't read too much into it. I was on a five-hour layover and needed something to do, so I got the ink. I like birds and I like fish. The bird looked cooler."

"Oh." I switch back to our original conversation. "So you're really not going to tell me what the deal is with Tiger and Proctor?"

"There's nothing to tell, Mia."

He's being short with me.

"Why are you annoyed?"

"I'm not annoyed."

"Mmm, I think you're keeping something from me. You've never been the best liar."

"I'm not lying. You're just trying to create drama where there is none."

"No worries, Bacchetti. I'll find out exactly what's going on when I go to the game Saturday."

Rush's neck stiffens.

"What game?"

"The one with Tiger. Remember, he invited me to that charity softball game at Yankee Stadium? It's this weekend."

I place a moist hot pad on Rush's left shoulder and neck and continue my ministrations of his muscles on the opposite side.

"I um, I didn't think you were still going to that," he says, almost tripping over his words. "I mean you haven't brought it up at all... at home."

"There was nothing to talk about it. It's not like it's some sort of big black-tie event or anything, which I'd love to go to one day by the way, hint-hint. Maybe you'll take me to the Espy Awards?"

"So you're going to go?"

"Why do you sound like that? Yes, I'm going to go. Is there a reason I shouldn't?"

There is silence between us as I remove the heating pad and place a new one on the other opposite side of his neck.

"I think it will be fun," I continue talking. "I haven't been to a softball game in years."

"And so you don't mind the entire locker room knowing that you're going out with him, but it's a problem if they know that we live together?"

I look around just to make sure no one is eavesdropping on our conversation, even though I know no one is scheduled to be in this room but us.

"Seriously, Rush?"

I remove the heating pad again and continue kneading his shoulders to loosen up any tightness I feel. He has massive trapezoids like many ballers, but they especially taut today.

"If someone compares me going to a ball game with him and living with you, which one is the more juicer piece of gossip? Which one is going to make players question if I got this job on by laying on my back? You're the one who taught me that."

"I think people know you're not that type of woman now, Mia. You're respected. The players like you."

"I haven't been on staff long enough for you to know that for sure. Plus, I'm twenty-five years old and haven't been on a proper date in months. And especially with this new job, I will meet no one at a bar or a club. I spend all of my time with the team, so it's pretty clear that eventually I'm going to end up in a romantic relationship with either an NFL player or someone on the staff. It's where I spend most of my time."

"You're right. You probably will end up with someone on the Nighthawks."

"Exactly, so I might as well start with him. He's been one of the nicer players to me since I started working here."

Rush's neck tenses again.

"Is there something else you want to say?" I ask him.

"Just be careful, Bird."

"Don't worry, *paw-paw*. I always am."

MIA

THE EVENT that Tiger takes me to is a charity baseball game. When we arrive, he is greeted by every celebrity in the place with adulation and warmth. I'm learning that while he may not be a marquee name in the averaged American household, he is much beloved by his peers and in the Hollywood scene. A fact he seems to revel in.

"You know a lot of people," I comment.

"Shh, it's a secret, but I would love to be cast in a movie one day."

"You want to act?"

"One day, after football is over, I've got to do something with my life."

"For sure. There's nothing wrong with planning for your second act early."

"What about you? Could you see yourself living somewhere else? Maybe working for another team one day clear across the country?"

"I just got this job." I smile.

"Yeah, but now that you're in, you could probably work for any NFL team you wanted."

"I never thought about it, but you're right. I could probably make a move one day. Hey, it's so cool that you're part of this charity event. Why aren't you playing?"

"I can't risk hurting myself playing a softball game. My body is my money maker."

I'm not sure that he would be risking much during a non-competitive softball game with actors, but okay.

"Oh, sure."

"Plus, I mean, this is not really my scene, anyway."

"Then why are we here?"

"It's a great photo opportunity. My publicist hooked it up."

"Your publicist?"

"Yeah, and right now it's all about serving good looks on the 'gram. A photo here should definitely get me some major likes today."

Unlike the rest of my generation, I've never been a huge social media follower. Neither is Rush. We just think it's kind of silly how a generation of people base their worth on how much validation they receive from strangers online. It's the oddest phenomenon.

"Oh, is your Instagram following big?"

"It's better than my Twitter following. I've got the third biggest following out of all the Nighthawks on the starter squad, but it could be better. You don't follow me there?"

Seriously?

"Uh, no."

"Then we should. Let's follow each other now."

"I only have a Facebook and Pinterest account. I never got an Instagram or Twitter started."

He stares at me as if I've just spoken an alien language.

"Say what? No Instagram?"

"I used to work at a university. I didn't want the students digging into my business online."

My excuse is total bullshit, but I've been giving that excuse so long I'm believing it myself.

"Oh, that makes sense, but you know you can create a brand on Instagram without having to post personal stuff."

"A brand? I don't think I have a brand. I'm a physical therapist by day and a bad karaoke singer by night."

"A lot of therapists have a brand. You could have your own You Tube channel describing different PT techniques and modalities. You could help current PT students. You could be a celebrity PT and take pics with all the players to build up your credibility."

"Wow, you're really into this."

"You have to be these days if you want to stay relevant."

"That sounds exhausting."

"You'll get used to it. How about I help you set up your Insta one day after dinner? I can even help you plan your first five posts. It will be easy."

"Let me think about it."

"Sure," he says, but I can tell he was hoping I'd jump at his offer.

Tiger seems really invested in the type of self-promotion that is totally understandable for someone in his position, but it's just not my jam.

A member of the publicity staff for the organization throwing the event approaches us at our seats.

"Ready for the group photo, Tiger?"

"Want to take it with me, Mia?"

The publicist looks at me and instantly I know that's not the picture she's hoping for. I'm a nobody.

"You go ahead. I don't want to steal your thunder," I jest.

"You're right," he chuckles in response. "You're too gorgeous for your own good."

While Tiger takes his photos, I scarf down a hot dog and half of a Dr. Pepper. Rush would be appalled, but it tastes damn good to eat some junk for once.

After the photos, I watch Tiger take a few selfies with some celebrity participants and a few kids who are spectators. He's personable and polite and has the whole thing down to a science. He's nothing like Rush, who can barely crack a smile for a fan and who's severely uncomfortable with notoriety.

And who's someone I sorely miss right now.

Tiger jogs back over, plops down on the seat, and immediately lifts his phone in the air.

"Lets take a flick, Mia."

"Sure."

"Let me show you how easy this is," he says, referring to our earlier conversation.

He leans into my shoulder and takes a few photos of us. I smile and make sure to flash some teeth, hoping that I look as if I'm having a good time.

"Which one do you like?" he asks.

I point to the picture that looks as if I'm enjoying myself the most and in a matter of seconds, Tiger puts a filter on it, texts the photo to me, and then posts it to his Instagram. Another minute later, he already gets thirty likes.

"See! There are some people that see all of my posts the minute they go live. Now if we give it a little longer, we should double those likes by the time we leave here. I'm just mad that I couldn't tag you. If you had an account, I'd be able to tag your name and people would follow you too. Want to do an Instagram story?"

Seriously, at this point, I just want to watch the damn

game. I didn't tag along on this date to get a crash course in social media.

"Whatever you want," I say.

He's actually pleased with my answer. Totally clueless to the subtext.

"We don't have to force it. We can wait until something natural happens."

"Cool."

The game gets underway, and it's pretty entertaining. Let's just say that most sitcom actors and actresses don't have an athletic bone in their bodies.

"Holy crap, is that the guy from the *Cambridge Witches* show on Netflix?"

"Yeah, that's him. He's a cool dude. You want to meet him?"

"Well, I'm not really the groupie type."

"There's nothing groupie-ish about a fan wanting to say hello. Celebrities appreciate it because there's nothing worse than being forgotten."

"Rush doesn't like it."

"Well... Rush is a little different than the average celebrity."

I hear a twinge of something when Tiger says Rush's name that I never noticed before.

"Do you have a problem with Rush?"

"No, but I definitely think he has a problem with me."

"Why would you say that?"

"I don't talk behind my teammates' backs, and this is just between us, but Rush threatened me with bodily harm if I didn't stay away from you."

His own teammate?

"That doesn't sound like him."

"I know it sounds out of character for him, which is why I let that shit go, but it definitely happened."

"Wow, I'm sorry about that. Rush is kind of overprotective when it comes to me. He's been that way since school."

I make an excuse for Rush's behavior, but I'm actually embarrassed by this news. I'm not sure how I'm going to earn the respect I want and need from my clients if Rush is going to go around and threaten them all to stay away from me. I decide to worry about that later. Right now, I want to enjoy myself.

Tiger introduces me to Bradley Kingman, who is the lead actor of the show I love. He is polite and sweet and we take a quick selfie that I will treasure forever. Although I'm annoyed with Mandy, I send her the picture too because I know how much she admires him as an actor. She doesn't respond to any of my texts, not even with a thumbs up emoji, but her read receipts are on so I always know when she's seen it.

All in all, it was a nice day out, something different, and I had a relatively good time with Tiger. He was respectful and fun to be around and even though any woman would have been ecstatic about this date; I realize that there was something missing.

A spark.

That thing that clicks when you're with someone new and shiny.

The twinkle I always feel with Rush.

MIA

I'm clearly still uncomfortable with telling anyone at work that I live with Rush, which is why I took the train and met Tiger in front of Yankee Stadium. The problem now is that he wants to drive me home and of course that can't happen, so I improvise and have him drop me off in front of my old building.

"I won't see you until Monday, Tiger, because I have tomorrow off. Thanks for a great day out. I had fun."

"Scott gave you a day off?"

"Yeah, the PT team is rotating Sundays off."

"Nice. So, Mia, I had a great time today too. You're so unpretentious and down to earth, just like I knew you'd be. Is it okay if I call you tomorrow?"

"Umm," I look down at the ground, not sure how to answer. I don't want to lead him on if there's no future for us, but I also don't want to make a big deal out of a simple phone call.

"Sure, if you want. I'll just be catching up on laundry all day."

"Cool." A satisfied smile spreads across his face.

Tiger sits in the car and waits for me to enter the vestibule of the building. Luckily, a woman and her pug are coming out for a walk, and so I'm able to enter. If she hadn't come downstairs, my plan would have unraveled, because you need a key to enter the main door. I wave as I pretend to walk towards the elevator and Tiger finally pulls off.

There's no mode of public transportation that can take me from this side of Jersey to Rush's house, so I'll need a car. I wait for a few moments to make sure Tiger's gone, and then I order an Uber.

I'm disappointed to find that Rush's Range Rover isn't parked in the driveway when I arrive home, but on the bright side that means I have a few moments to unwind before he inevitably grills me about my day out at the ballpark.

I'm still wound a little tight from the long day and the whole ridiculous stunt I just pulled with Tiger, so I pop open one of the beers I have hidden in the produce drawer of the fridge.

"Michael, play *Shadow Dancing* by Andy Gibb."

Playing *Shadow Dancing* by Andy Gibb.

I'm snapping my fingers as I sing. It's another good song, but this time by their baby brother. Maybe Rush is onto something with liking this family of singers. Their harmonies are really phenomenal.

The bop of the song feels sexy and my mind wanders off into an imaginative place where I fantasize about my best friend and yoga poses. I literally start to ache for him, or at least for the *idea* of him and what it could possibly be like between us.

I climb the stairs to my room and fall on my bed and

play out different scenarios in my head. Maybe the next time we try couple poses, I'll abandon all subtleties and purposely fall right on his dick.

I open the small suitcase under my bed and reach for one of my favorite vibrators. I name my plants and even some of my crystals, but naming my vibrators is where I draw the line, so it's just model 274-3. At the time, I spent what felt like an exorbitant amount of money on it from a Sharper Image catalog and it's been with me the longest. It doesn't have all the bells and whistles like some of my other vibrators, but it always gets the job done and will probably still be functioning long after the zombie apocalypse. Nothing can break this bad boy.

I ask Michael to play *Red Light Special* by TLC on repeat, then I slide under the covers and close my eyes as the loud hum of the vibrator between my legs lulls me into a relaxed state.

When the door to my room suddenly opens, I scream. "Aaaah!!!"

Rush is standing at the doorway with a scowl on his face.

I immediately turn off the vibrator and slide it deeper under the covers.

"Dammit, you scared me. Why didn't you knock?"

"I knocked."

His eyes glance at the bump under my blankets.

"Must have been an excellent date," he comments, his voice thick with fury.

"It was." I lie. "Next time knock harder before you just waltz in."

"Because you might be busy?"

This time he points to the concealed vibrator.

"Uh, yeah, I might be," I retort sarcastically. "Can't a girl masturbate in peace?"

He takes another step forward and stops to run his hand through his thick, dark tresses.

"You shouldn't be going on dates with Samuels," he says after a deep breath.

"I thought we talked about this. You can't protect from everything by keeping me from doing anything."

"That's not what I'm doing."

I slide one of my legs out from beneath the covers not only because it's hot but because I'm being passive aggressive as fuck. I want to see what Rush will do, if anything. He doesn't want me, but he doesn't want anyone else to have me either? Is that the game we're playing now?

"Then what are you doing, Rush?"

Rush glances at my leg and bites the corner of his lip.

"He's not serious, Mia."

"I don't expect a marriage proposal anytime soon, but Tiger seems serious enough to me."

"Don't call him that," he says through gritted teeth.

"That's his name."

"His name is fucking Samuels."

"I call him Tiger."

He's gotten so close to the edge of the bed now I can see the two blue veins in his neck pulsing. He hasn't been this angry with me in a long time, and I'm not even sure how we got here.

My heart is fluttering like the wings of a butterfly. I know exactly why, but I've been fighting it for so long I don't know what to do to tamper it down in this moment.

I've been dutifully by Rush's side for years and not because we're friends or because he's the only person I completely trust, but because subconsciously I've been waiting.

Waiting for him to see me.

Waiting for him to want me.

Waiting for him to choose me.

My eyes are wide as I pull the covers up closer to my chin. There's no farther I can run from him.

He leans in with his hands firmly tucked in his gray sweatpants pockets and takes a long whiff of my neck.

"You smell like hot dogs, grass, and the inside of his fucking car."

"Say what you have to say, Rush."

He holds up his phone.

"I saw an Instagram story of this cute new celebrity sports couple on a date."

He clicks Tiger's profile picture and his latest story pops up. It's a picture of me laughing with Bradley and Tiger, but the caption he added reads: **When your girl is star-struck for the first time:)**

"I didn't know," I mutter under my breath.

"You didn't know that you were his girl?" he asks in a raised voice.

"I didn't know that he posted that. Obviously, I'm not his girl."

"Is it obvious?"

His face contorts into a painful expression. He dips his head down and our foreheads meet with our eyes wide open, anchoring each other in place.

"Is it obvious?" he whispers again against my lips.

A sudden warm wetness gushes between my legs and I rub my feet together like a cricket to ease the ache at my core. Rush slowly peels the covers down my body as his eyes still hold mine in place.

I am exposed. Covered only by a bra and panties. He lazily rakes his eyes from my hair, to my breasts, to my waist, my crotch, my thighs and finally my toes.

When the air settles, I stare at him; he stares at me, and we both knew that everything is about to fucking change.

"The only fucking that's obvious is that you belong to me, Bird."

TWENTY-SIX

RUSH

I FEEL like a caged lion who's been freed from a self-imposed friend zone prison. Now that I'm out and have tasted a bit of the wilderness, I never want to go back to that place again.

Mia belongs to me, has always belonged to me, and it's time that we both own that shit.

Our tongues hungrily explore each other's mouths as I grind my hardened length into her panty covered pussy. I want her to feel how much and how long I've wanted her.

She's panting heavily once I release her lips, staring at me with warm tawny eyes that twinkle with flecks of copper. Her desire is needy but tentative. She may not be sure where this carnal need for each other is coming from or where it's headed, but I have enough clarity for the both of us.

"I can see your pretty little brain working overtime," I tell her. "You're trying to make sense of this. You're worried that this will ruin us. But you don't need to think that hard about this, Bird. Just let it happen."

"What are we doing, Rush?" Her whispered question is laced with lust.

"I'll show you exactly what we're doing."

I pick up the vibrator that she tried to hide from me down at the edge of the bed.

"We'll start with this," I tell her.

Her eyes widen.

"What are you doing?"

"Who were you thinking about when you were using this earlier?"

"No one."

Her eyes look away as if she's ashamed.

I turn the vibrator on low, and her eyes enlarge with trepidation. There's more than one way to get to the truth.

"Rush–"

"Spread your legs," I tell her.

"Rush, please–"

"And pull the crotch of your panties to the side."

Her breathing grows heavier with each command. I'm on the right track. Mia likes this.

"We can't," she says unconvincingly.

"Why?"

"It will change everything."

"I certainly hope so, Bird. I'm waiting."

Her creamy long legs slowly spread open as the buzz of the vibrator fills the room with erotic anticipation.

"The panties." I remind her.

She uses two of her delicate fingers to pull the crotch of her panties to the side.

"Good girl."

I waste no time and lower the vibrator right to her glistening clit.

Her back immediately arches.

I don't know how long she's been masturbating before I walked into the house, but she's already primed and ready to come so I have to be strategic about this.

I want Bird to fucking suffer.

I plan to bring her pretty ass right to the edge but not allow her to come as a punishment for the torture she's put me through today. All day I was on edge thinking about her date with Tiger. I wanted to stop her from going a million times, but worried I was being selfish.

How could I ask her to come live with me on the pretense of it being a safe space where she can get her life together and then suddenly profess some newfound romantic feelings for her?

That's not cool.

Especially if she doesn't reciprocate those feelings.

I could tell she was obviously attracted to me but did her feelings go beyond a physical craving, because this is way past that for me.

She leans her head back into the pillow and lifts her hips off the bed to surrender to the orgasm that's building inside of her. She looks so fucking beautiful as I lean in and initiate a kiss, which this time is slower, more languid, as I see the delicate muscles in her neck rise and fall.

When her kiss becomes more aggressive, I know that she's getting close to her release and I pull the vibrator away.

A soft whimper escapes from her mouth.

I stand up and watch her practically writhing on the bed with want.

Then I begin to slowly peel off of my clothes until I am completely bare, my dick swinging hard in the wind.

She rakes her eyes along every hard edge of my body and I can feel that she desires me. Good. If she can feel an ounce of how much I want her, then we're getting somewhere.

"You are beautiful, Rush."

I smile as a thank you but don't say a word.

I silently get in the bed next to her and kiss her again. She reaches for me this time. Grabbing me by the back of my neck as she passionately makes love to my mouth.

I turn the vibrator on again.

And she makes a small gasp.

"I want you," she says plainly.

"Not yet."

I place the vibrator between her legs again and she cries out.

"Rush!"

What started out as an exquisite punishment designed for her is turning into one for me. My dick angrily stiffens in between our bodies. It wants inside her in the worst way, but I need to do this right. I've waited so long for her today to return home to me where she belongs, that now I want to take all night to demonstrate why.

When she claws my shoulder, I pull the vibrator away again. A thin layer of sweat covers her body and her eyes look glazed. She looks like the most beautiful creature I've ever seen.

"Take your bra off," I tell her.

Before she even has a chance to take it completely off, my lips encircle and suck her left nipple. Her back arches again and her eyes roll to the back of her head. I make a mental note that my Bird likes nipple play.

"Turn over."

Mia flips over, and I prop a pillow underneath her hips so that her ass is up high. This has to be my favorite part of Mia's body. I ogle it for a minute and rub myself out as I do.

Right now is not about but my satisfaction but I had to relieve just a bit of the pressure building inside of me.

Now that she's had a moment to calm down, I flick the vibrator on one last time. I know she's not going to last much longer and at some point it would just be cruel to not let her come.

The hum is the only sound we hear between us when she finally says the words I've been waiting all day, or really for months to hear.

"I was thinking about you, Rush."

"Say what, Bird?"

"I was thinking about you inside of me when I was playing with myself today."

Fuck me.

I slide her panties to the side once more and settle the vibrator on her clit as I lightly begin to slap each of her ass cheeks.

"What were we doing in this fantasy?" I ask her, as I continue to taunt her pussy.

"We... you... oh my God. I'm *commmminggg!*"

I don't even recognize the wicked laughter that comes from my mouth as I watch Mia literally convulse, face down, ass up in the air, with an orgasm that is shattering her from head to toe.

It's a beautiful fucking thing to watch.

I could definitely get used to this.

MIA

I feel like I just ran a marathon. I am spent. Rush just gave me the best orgasm of my life and he hasn't even been inside of me yet. If this is what sex is going to be like with him, then sign me up for the lifetime plan. I guess this is what people mean when they say *it's always the quiet ones.*

I roll to my side and stare at the immense man suddenly standing by my bed like he's some sort of brand new kind of superhero. Thor on steroids. He's staring down at me and holding a condom in his hand.

"Do you want to roll it on or should I, Bird?"

Damn, he's sexy.

His dick is jutting toward me like a raging bull in desperate need to be put out of its misery, so I put it exactly where it seems to want to go first.

Inside of my mouth.

Rush inhales swiftly as I wrap my lips around the tip, then he kneels down on the bed so I can swallow him deeper inside my mouth. I close my eyes for a second to relax the muscles in my throat. Rush is thick and long and his big dick is going to take some getting use to.

Once my throat opens a bit more and I find a rhythm, I suck him off so good that he slaps one of my hands against the wall to brace himself.

"Shit, Bird."

"Hmmm?" I hum a little with his dick still in my mouth.

His body shivers.

He loves it.

When I think he's had enough, I release the suction and lick the underside of his cock from root to tip with a wanton look of a stone cold seductress.

I feel like a formidable goddess.

Maybe my moon is in Venus.

Or maybe I'm just finally having sex with the right man.

"Take your panties off, Bird."

I lick the corner of my lips as if just tasted the most delicious treat of my life and look at him with brand new clarity.

"Ok, Rush."

He lowers himself back on the bed, hovering above me, and it creaks underneath our weight.

"I think you liked my dick in your mouth," he says, as he slides his fingers between my folds and feels the slickness there.

Before I can respond with one of my witty comebacks, he captures my mouth with his and simultaneously slides two of my fingers inside of me.

"Damn," I moan into his mouth.

"You're so fucking wet, Mia. This better be all for me."

I slide both of my hands in his hair and grab it in by the roots.

"It is, dummy."

Rush lets out a laugh. Only the two of us could still crack jokes in the middle of making love for the first time.

He pauses for a moment to stare at me. I'm not sure if he's second guessing the next step we're about to take, but I wait and play it by ear. We've done a lot tonight, but it's not too late to stop this from going any further if he wants to.

"You're gorgeous, Bird. Fucking gorgeous."

I smile, relieved at the sentiment.

"You're gorgeous too."

"Spread your legs wide for me," he orders, with a quick slap on one of my ass cheeks. "I'm a big boy and you're going need to make room for me."

I quirk my lips in anticipation and spread my legs. I want more than I've ever wanted anyone in my life.

Before he enters me, he pays homage to my pussy and kisses the insides of my thighs, above my mound, and all around my core. My entire body literally hums with pleasure as he methodically teases and licks my clit, all while keeping one of my nipples tightly rolled between two of his fingers.

I don't think I can survive another fifteen minutes of his exquisite torture. My pussy aches and I want him so badly that I can't wait any longer.

"I need you to fuck me, Rush." I say bluntly, as I use one of my fingers to trace the pulsing bird tattoo on his neck. "Please."

He rolls me to one side, facing him, then places my leg with the bad knee on top of him. As he pushes just the tip of his dick inside of me, I savor the moment.

"This is going to change everything, Rush," I tell him.

"I know."

My hand cradles the side of his beautiful face, pulling him in for a slow, lazy kiss as we continue our descent out of platonic friendship and into a much more dangerous place of love.

I'm the type of girl who believes in karma, signs, fate, and destiny. Whatever life throws my way, I just roll with it because I know it's my divine right.

But this.

This almost feels like cheating fate.

I have always been lucky to be Rush's friend, but I never dared to imagine that we'd be anything more.

Rush grips my leg and rests it higher over his hip as he continues to enter me.

"Damn, you're tight."

He exhales harshly as he enters my tight pussy. The sensation of being penetrated by him is exquisite and feels frighteningly intimate. I close my eyes as our kissing grows increasingly carnal.

"Your pussy feels so fucking good, Bird. Eyes on me, baby."

Rush hikes my leg up a little higher, which allows him to seat himself balls deep inside of me. I am stuffed and stretched and I've never felt better.

In the past, I could only imagine how big Rush's dick was underneath his clothes or by the large bulge I'd seen from time to time through his sweats, but he's so huge that I need to take a moment to adjust to the size of him.

"You like it, baby?"

I can tell he is purposefully being as gentle with me as possible, but I don't want gentle. I want more.

"Yes, Rush, but give me more of you and faster."

"Shit, okay."

He grips my ass cheek firmly and starts driving himself harder into me. Each punishing stroke makes my pussy vibrate. I kiss him harder this time with a newfound self-realization that I've probably always wanted this man since the day we met.

He's mine.

My heart knew it.

That's why it held on so tight.

Keeping the cluckers away while I made myself the center of his life.

Damn, I'm a sinister boss bitch!

"Get out of your head, Bird, and keep your eyes on me while I make you come," Rush instructs with a devilish grin on his face.

"Or maybe I'll make you come," I tease.

He pounds my pussy harder.

"Or maybe we come together," he grunts, gripping my ass tightly.

Little white fireworks pop behind my pupils as I blissfully come hard and fast together with Rush. I lay splayed on my back with my arms extended wide and totally exhausted.

"That was something," I say.

"Sure as shit was."

"You are amazing in bed," I readily admit out loud.

"So are you, Bird."

"We probably should have tried this a long time ago."

He grins and clasps my hand tenderly.

"Maybe we should have."

We puff in silence for a moment longer, and then I turn my face to his.

"Rush?"

"Yes, baby."

"Let's do it again."

TWENTY-EIGHT

MIA

PRESEASON

I'm not sure how he talked me into it this, but Rush and I are driving to the practice field together in his gas guzzling, Fuji white, Range Rover instead of the green goblin. Admittedly, my car is a bit slower than his on the highway and maybe his seats are a kind of buttery, but I never thought I'd betray my little car like this. She's been very good to me. I ain't going to lie though, these couple of weeks living a pampered life with Rush has been something special.

He has a chef service that comes to his house, prepares him fresh meals (for both of us now) and then packages them per meal and per day, then puts them in the fridge or freezer for us to just in pop in the oven when we're ready to eat. Every meal without fail has been delicious except for the butternut squash soup. I'm not a big fan of the weird orange vegetable, but Rush seems to love it.

It's also been pleasurable to come home from a day of

work and find that the entire house has been immaculately cleaned, not an item out of place, and nothing stolen (which was my first fear when Rush said a cleaning service would also have access to my stuff). I may not have much, but the few things I own mean the world to me, like the diamond earrings Rush bought me or my Grandmom's hand-stitched initialed handkerchief.

Finally, and the grandest perk of all, is that when I get an urge to be touched, or held, or fucked… I've got in-house dick at my beck and call.

Phenomenal dick.

The way he bends and stretches me in unyielding positions and makes me come while I'm in them? He has no idea the power that he now yields over me now. I'm his sex slave and he doesn't even know it. Some nights I have to talk myself down so that I'm not the one initiating sex all the damn time, because hey, a girl would like her bones jumped too.

"You want to stop for coffee?" he asks.

"They have all of that at the food commons at the training center."

"Yeah, but we have to act like friends there. Here we can actually act like a normal couple."

My heart melts just a little.

A normal couple.

Rush is the most romantic man I've ever met, and he isn't even trying to be.

"Okay."

We stop at a local coffee shop and sit next to each other on one side of the dark wooden table. With his hood up on his head, and how early it is, chances are likely that no one will recognize him. The only thing which can sometimes be a giveaway is his size. Men his size are often groomed at a young age to play a sport, so naturally people stare at first to see. Is he someone famous?

I drink my coffee with cream and two sugars and he drinks a protein smoothie and we chat about irrelevant stuff that most couples do and it feels really... right.

"We should probably start thinking about what we're going to do with your room."

"What do you mean?"

"Well, you haven't slept in it much."

"Do you want me to go back to it?"

I give him a quick peck on his succulent lips.

"Hilarious, Bird." He taps my nose with his pointer finger. "I'm just saying that at this point it isn't your bedroom anymore. You sleep with me now because that's where you belong."

"I don't think we have to do anything with the room. My blue sofa likes it in there just fine."

"It's the second biggest bedroom in the house. Maybe we should make it your office or something. I mean, you are my house manager and all."

"Which, by the way, I think you could cut your costs down enormously by making a few adjustments. The landscapers don't need to come every week. Grass doesn't grow that damn fast. They can come twice a month. And what's up with that koi pond?"

"What about it?"

"You already have fish in the aquarium in the house."

"And I have fish in my yard too."

"It costs a fortune to maintain it, and for what? You have zero time to sit out there and enjoy it."

"I have the off season."

"It's freezing in New Jersey in March and April."

"The pond stays."

"Ugh, fine."

"I see you like to live on a lean budget."

"Getting rid of a pond is living lean?"

"You know what I mean."

"It's just that I know what it's like not to have enough money to pay the bills when you feel like just a few moments ago you had it. I don't want you to pay for the upkeep of this pond, and ten years from now you wonder where all your money went. I've seen the ball player financial horror stories on television."

"I'm not trying to brag, Bird, but trust me when I say that I make enough money to afford this lifestyle for the rest of my life if I'm careful with my money."

"The key word is careful."

"I've put a large portion of my income into investments that I have my parents watching with a very close eye. I even bought some popular Tesla stock before it doubled in price."

"Tesla?"

"Yep."

"But you drive a Range Rover."

"Which the Tesla dividends paid for." He chuckles.

"I'll make a conservationist out of you yet."

"Yeah, good luck with that."

The two of us hold hands between the seats the entire time we ride to work. It's cute and romantic and feels kind of odd... but at the same time absolutely right.

He exits the car and opens the passenger door for me, holding my hand to help me out. My knee is bothering me today, so it's a little difficult to step down out of his truck without help. As we grow closer toward the training center, Rush still hasn't let go of my hand as I try tugging it away.

"Bird, if you let go of my hand I'll toss your ass over my shoulder and walk you into work myself."

"You wouldn't dare."

"You know I would."

I try tugging my hand away again.

"You must want everyone to know that I made you come literally eight hours ago."

Although our relationship has changed over the last two weeks, I still think it's best to keep our business and personal lives as separate as we can for now.

"They'll definitely know if we walk inside the building holding hands. I told you we shouldn't of done it doggy-styled. My knee was fine until last night."

"So you're blaming me? You physically stuck your ass so far in my face that I could smell how much you wanted me, and you know very well that your juicy ass and that wet pussy are my two weaknesses."

"Lower your voice." I hush him.

"And I was playing around with you last night," I chastise him. "I didn't think you would slap my ass and fuck me senseless over a beanbag chair in the den."

"I heard zero complaints last night. In fact, all I heard was harder, Rush, deeper, Rush." He chuckles almost sinisterly.

I tug my hand again, and he pulls his in the other direction.

"Which do you prefer, Bird? Your crutches are in your office and the cane is at home. I can carry you in or you can walk into work with some dignity, take some Motrin, and get on with your day."

I huff in total exasperation and stop fighting.

"Hold it tighter," he demands.

I clasp his hand tighter.

"That's better."

It's preseason now, which means that the players aren't doing training drills every day but are practicing game plays as a team. Most of the players are gearing up for morning practice at this time of day and the trainers are probably in the therapy rooms, so I'm hoping that no one will even see Rush helping me to my office. Of course, things can never be that easy for me. Once we enter the inner courtyard of the training center, the first person we see is Miranda.

Her eyes immediately drop to our hands and I release his just as quickly.

"Morning, Miranda," he says in an all business voice.

"Morning, Rush."

"Let me get your crutches for you, Mia." He says to me without skipping a beat and then he strides off toward the PT office, leaving me in the hallway with the woman we both embarrassed just a couple of weeks ago.

What do I say to her?

She cocks her head to the side as if she knows I'm struggling with a way to break the tension. "Good Morning, Mia."

A woman can often read body language, subtext and subtleties, and the tone Miranda used to say good morning to me is all I need to hear to know that she now sees me as a threat and not an ally. If there was any question before, it's been answered. Miranda still has a thing for Rush.

"Morning, Miranda."

"Your knee seems to be a very temperamental thing. One day you're walking around just fine and other days you need... help."

What a bitch.

"It's the rain."

"But it's not raining outside."

"Not right now, but I promise you, there's definitely a storm coming."

And I'm not talking about the weather.

"Ah, yes," she agrees. "There probably is."

TWENTY-NINE

MIA

"THIS IS AN INCREDIBLY STUPID IDEA."

"I don't think it is."

"There are over hundred-and-twenty-five people on this campus at any given time. Someone could find us in here." I giggle as Rush bends down to yank my sweatpants down.

"Put your hands on my shoulders and step out of the pants while I'm being a gentleman about this shit."

My core clenches with each dirty command that Rush gives me. My desire for this man grows with each passing day, and it's even surprising me.

He falls to his knees, grabs me behind my thighs, and pulls me forward.

"Damn you smell good."

I slide one of my hands in his thick mane and grip some of the strands taut at the roots. Then he takes my pussy with his mouth and ravenously feasts. It doesn't take long for my clit to swell and my core to burst from the rushed orgasm that consumes me.

"Fuck, Rush."

He licks the corner of his mouth and smiles.

"You taste like fucking sunshine and strawberries."

He stands and kisses me hard. I can taste myself on his tongue and wish we could take this a bit further, but we're acting like two horny teenagers with no responsibilities. We both have work to get back to.

"We've got to go," I say.

"Funny how you say that after you got your shit off."

"Nobody told you to start something that we couldn't finish."

"That's not true, baby. I'm booked for a sixty-minute therapy session with you and we've only been in here for fifteen."

"You're so greedy. I'll give you a ten-minute blow job and then we're out of here."

"Uh-uh, I want inside of that pussy."

"Rush, please," I (sort of) protest.

He takes a condom out of his pocket, slides down his shorts, and rolls the piece of rubber on in record time. I bite my lip in anticipation, although I'm a little wary of doing this. I may be a free spirit about some things, but I'm not the hugest risk taker in other ways. I know. It's one of the biggest enigmas about my entire personality.

When he's ready, Rush lifts me in the air and against the wall. My legs instinctively circle around his waist and my arms around his neck.

"Whose pussy does this belong to?"

"Yours."

"That's right. Which means I can have it any fucking time I want it."

"Yes," I feebly admit.

"Then I'm taking what's mine right now."

His dick is hard and ready and feels like a big ass cucumber when he first rams it inside of me. I squeeze my eyelids tight and bite his shoulder to keep from crying out. He works himself into a sweat as he plunges his thick length inside my pussy over and over with deep punishing strokes.

"I'm coming, Bird. Fuck, you feel good."

I squeal as another orgasm coils inside of me

"I love... I love the way you fuck me," I say, totally saving me from the blunder that was about to come out of my mouth.

Who says I love you to someone in a damn supply closet, Mia?

Rush comes with a deep growl of relief and my second orgasm comes chasing right after his. We're both panting heavily when he lowers me back to the ground so I can put my clothes back on. He rolls off the condom, ties it off, and is about to toss it in the trash can when I stop him.

"What are you doing?"

"Throwing it out."

"Uh-uh."

I grab a piece of office paper and wrap the condom like a Christmas gift, then slide it into the pocket of his shorts.

"What in the ever loving hell are you doing, Mia?"

"You can't toss this in an office trashcan. First, that shit is gross and second, I can't have your DNA exposed for any crafty little clucker to find and shove up her vagina with a turkey baster."

"Seriously, Mia? You watched too many soap operas when you were young. No one does shit like that. That's why it makes for great television."

"Desperate women will do way more devious things than that. Just toss it in one of the large receptacles outside on the grounds. Better to be safe than sorry."

"You're crazy, baby." He kisses me ardently on the lips. "But you haven't steered me wrong all these years, so I'll do it. I just can't believe I'm carrying my own jizz in my pocket."

"If you don't want some crazy baby mama one day, you'll thank me."

"Hell, I think I already see one of those crazy baby mamas in my future."

***

Rush and I wasted too much time fucking around to get any of his actual therapy done, and Darius had to cancel his session for some added time with one of the offensive coaches, so I'm sitting in the main office getting some paperwork done which there's lots of. I guess when the owner is paying players millions of dollars to win ball games; they want an accurate paper trail of all injuries and therapies.

It only takes me twenty minutes to input my notes into the computer system, so I decide to look for Scott and see if there's anything else he may want my help with. I'm suddenly invigorated with newfound energy after my freaky romp in the closet.

I see Rush on the practice field and was going to go over and say something dirty in his ear when Miranda walks up to him. I haven't seen her since that awkward morning in the courtyard, but it definitely appears as if they've seen each other since.

I can't hear anything from the distance I'm standing, but I can guess by their body language that she's telling him some sort of story. She's flapping her hands, switching her weight between both feet, and the most interesting part about this entire exchange is that she's also smiling from ear to ear. She's not angry or indifferent with him. In fact, she's dare I say happy to be talking to the man I just fucked less than an hour ago.

And holy cheese balls... Rush doesn't look irritated or uncomfortable with the conversation either. In fact, he just smiled, and not the type of half-ass smile he gives a clucker, but the kind that is usually reserved for me.

"Whatcha looking at?"

Tiger startles me when he walks up behind me. I turn and plaster on a fake smile.

"Nothing, what's up with you?"

Tiger is not the type of man to take no for an answer, so I had to have a conversation with him after Rush and I started sleeping together. I obviously didn't tell him anything about us, so I gave him the not wanting to mix work with personal speech. He didn't buy it for one second, but I think it's safe to say he's okay.

We were definitely not a love match.

"About to do some sprints," he answers.

"Mmm, okay. Make sure you stretch first."

He looks over at Rush and Miranda talking. She just touched his arm.

"Hmm, they look cozy," Tiger comments.

"Who, them?"

He points toward them as if I hadn't been staring down their throats this whole time.

"I'd bet one-hundred bucks that they're still hooking up."

"Still?" I pretend to have no knowledge of Rush and Miranda's past relationship.

"Those two used to bump uglies big time. The entire squad knew it."

"Really? I'm surprised something like that got out. Rush is pretty quiet about his private life."

"It's hard for things to stay quiet around here. Most of us are barely out of college. Women, cars and football are all we talk, eat, shit and breathe most days. I even heard he was thinking about marrying her."

My stomach rolls.

Did he just say Rush was thinking about marrying Miranda?

I don't fucking believe it.

Rush would have told me something that important.

"But I'm sure you already knew that being his friend and all."

I'm so shocked with this rumor that I don't take in account that Tiger might be fishing for information instead of telling me facts and I fall for it hook, line and sinker.

"Yeah, I knew," I say, lying through my teeth.

"Oh, so it was true? Damn, Bacchetti is one sneaky fucker, but I understand why. It's better to keep something like that under wraps. Miranda is definitely Grade A Wifey material."

"Yeah." My heart breaks a little. "She is."

THIRTY

MIA

Tonight, Rush had to stay at camp longer for a meeting, so I've penciled in some time to earn my keep around here and do the job of managing his house. It's the first time I've been alone in the house in a long time with nothing but the fish and the Michael AI to keep me company.

"Michael, play *Would I Lie To You* by the Eurythmics."

Playing *Would I Lie To You* by the Eurythmics.

It's a dangerous thing for me to be left to my own thoughts, because when I am, I reflect on the conversation between Rush and Miranda. I decided not to ask him about it. It was just a conversation and it would make me look incredibly insecure. The man is allowed to talk to whoever he wants, especially if he's at work. Who am I to question it?

Then I think about the conversation she overheard between Rush and I in the hallway the day I was hired. She couldn't have been too happy with him after hearing the things he said. Yet there they were, chatting it up like they were old school chums.

And then there's the bomb that Tiger dropped.

Was Rush actually in a serious relationship with Miranda and lied to me about it? Why would his teammates think he was going to propose if there was no validity to that story? In my experience, where there's smoke there's most definitely fire.

Although the previous house manager organized all of Rush's monthly bill payments to deduct automatically from his main checking account, I cautioned him to monitor it anyway. He agreed and gave me his banking information. Once a month I log in just to keep track of outgoing payments and to make sure that there aren't any questionable charges.

I log in his account and scroll through the transaction history. Everything looks normal except for one noticeable difference. There's a charge for $125 to a flower delivery service and last time I checked it wasn't Mother's Day and I received nothing. But there could a million reasons for this. Maybe he surprised his mom with flowers. Maybe he sent them to a sick friend. I can't start playing this game with myself. The reason why our friendship has always worked is that it was built on a bedrock of trust. I will not ruin it now.

The next day Rush and I ride together to work. I'm not angry or anything, but he can tell that there's a part of me that's distant.

"You, okay?"

"Yeah, I'm good."

"Did you and the surgeon decide on a date for the procedure?"

Rush thinks it's my knee that's bothering me. Maybe that's for the best.

"If you guys win this season, then the surgery won't be

until the offseason. If you guys go home early and don't make the playoffs, I may push it up earlier."

"And you're sure you like this surgeon?"

"Yeah, why?"

"It's your third surgery. They can't open up your knee a fourth time to correct mistakes. I just want to make sure that you have the best that money can buy this time, so it's the last time."

"I did my homework. This guy is one of the best. I'm confident that he can patch me up."

"Okay."

He doesn't seem pleased with my answer.

"Will you let me at least be there?" He asks.

"Of course, Rush."

"Okay."

We're both quiet for a moment before he brings up another long running topic of conversation between us.

"Did you decide what you want to do with the bedroom?"

"I hadn't given it much thought."

"I thought we decided on an office."

"You decided on an office."

"Well, that's why I'm asking what you want to do with it?" He taps his palm on the steering wheel with frustration.

"Why are you getting upset with me, dude?"

"Don't call me dude."

"I've been calling you that since we were eighteen-years-old."

"But we're *fucking* now."

He puts emphasis on the word fucking and somehow it doesn't sound as sexy as it usually does but instead sounds distant and cold.

I don't want to talk to him anymore, so I lean into the

passenger door, look outside the window, and hum the melody to *Beautiful Day* by U2 until we get to work.

*****

Usually my days fly by, but work trudges by for the first time since I've started with the Nighthawks. Rush and I have never had a serious argument before, but I think this morning in the Rover may have been our first. I don't feel good about it, but I also know that I have a job to do, and I'll get the opportunity to address it later. We do still live together. Eventually I'll have to talk to him and clear the air.

"Hey, Mia, Human Resources needs to see you today."

"They need me to go to the office?"

"Yeah, something about more forms."

"Okay."

This is not the best day in the world for me to see Miranda, but I know she spends most her day in that office with two other people. She's more than likely going to be there when I go up there. I just have to pull up my big girl panties and handle it.

"Hi, Mia, Miranda's in her office waiting for you."

"Oh, I thought it was just some papers I had to sign or something."

"Um, I'm not really sure everything that she needs. Just knock once and go inside."

"Cool."

I knock twice and Miranda answers.

"Come in."

"Afternoon, Miranda."

"Afternoon, Mia. Have a seat."

"What's this about?"

She plops three envelopes on top of her desk.

I sent some information concerning your health insurance to your house, and they were returned to sender. I thought we should straighten it out before the tax forms go out later in the year.

At this point, I'm droning out all of her words, because my eyes are affixed to the extravagant and relatively fresh purple flower arrangement on top of the table behind her. She notices my point of focus and paints the smallest of smirks across her face.

"They're beautiful, aren't they?"

"They match your hair."

"Yes, I guess they do. Beautiful and thoughtful."

"Is it your birthday?"

"No."

"Did someone die?"

"Excuse me?"

"Was there a death in your family?"

"No, just a *stormy* day."

Her reference to our last conversation doesn't escape me.

She taps the envelopes impatiently. "Your address, Mia? Can we update the records, please?"

I stare at her quietly for a moment and I can sense the ring of smug satisfaction floating around her head like a halo.

"My bad," I say. "I should have updated it earlier."

I write my new address on the lavender sticky notepad on her desk in black marker.

2090 Hanaway Drive

Alpine, New Jersey

The look on her face is priceless.

She knows exactly who lives there.

I pick up my envelopes off the desk and walk to the door.

"Have a great day."

I exit her office with my head held high, but all the while I'm simmering underneath.

Why did Rush buy her those fucking purple flowers?

Tonight is the night I'm going to get all the answers I need.

MIA

Our schedules are different now because we're in preseason, so after a strenuous practice, Rush can leave if he has no other meetings or therapies. I, on the other hand, have to stay to work with the players on my rotation.

When I arrive home, Rush has already set the dining room table and warmed one of our gourmet dinners. I guess he had the same plan in mind because we desperately need to talk.

"Grab a shower and we can have dinner."

"Cool."

The soothing water gives me a moment to regroup and consider what I'm going to say. This thing with Miranda is eating me alive. It's making me question why I ever thought it was a good idea to take a job at the same workplace as Rush, and it's also making me consider how Rush is a much more complicated person than I ever knew.

I loosen my ponytail and let my waves free. I lotion my body then put on my fluffy green robe that I basically pulled out of a mean woman's hands during a Black Friday sale. A very proud moment, if I do say so myself. My knee is killing me, so I grab my cane out of the bedroom and head downstairs. Stress is a trigger for inflammation in the body and the last few days have been tense.

We're having gluten-free lobster mac and cheese, green beans and grilled blue fish for dinner. It's delicious, but every swallow feels like it's two seconds away from getting stuck in my throat.

"So I thought we should talk," Rush breaks the ice.

"Okay."

He chews and swallows a few of his green beans, takes a deep breath and starts.

"Bird, I can feel you pulling away from me and I don't know why."

"You're feeling is way off the mark."

"Then explain it to me. Did I do something wrong?"

"No."

"Then what's going on?"

"This is just harder than I thought it would be."

"In what way?"

"I'm an open book most of the time, but this clandestine relationship we're in is taking a toll on me. I don't think I'm built for it."

"We can tell the whole fucking team if you want. Tomorrow if we need to. It's not a secret for me."

"Are you sure?"

"What do you mean, am I sure? I'm not the one still holding onto the whole narrative that we're college friends. That's you."

"Because you're the one who advised me to keep it quiet. I followed your lead."

"That was at first."

"Well, I can't keep up with you and how all the rules keep changing."

He places his fork down quietly on the table and anchors his forearms on top of it.

"What rules keep changing?"

"Did you send someone flowers this week?" I blurt out, getting to the crux of what's really going on.

He raises one of his eyebrows out of curiosity.

"How do you know that?"

"The charge was on your account. Remember, it's my job to notice out-of-place things like that."

"Yes, I sent someone flowers."

"Someone like who?"

"Does it matter?"

"Dodgy much? Yeah, I think it fucking matters."

"I sent them to Miranda."

"Finally, the truth."

"I always tell you the truth."

"Are you fucking her?"

"What did you just say?!"

"I asked you if you are putting your dick inside the purple people eater's vagina. Is that a clear enough question for you?"

"You don't trust me, Bird?"

He has the nerve to look hurt.

"Stop answering my questions with a question."

He lifts his fork back up and angrily takes a bite of his Mac and cheese. Glaring at me with every chew.

"Did you know the entire team knows you were sleeping with her?" I ask him.

"I didn't care."

"Oh, is that fucking so! You didn't care at all if the world knew that you were with the formidable Miranda Green."

"Because she had nothing to lose, Mia. Her cousin is the

general manager. She'll never get fired. Not unless he gets fired first."

Oops, I didn't know that.

"My silence about our ever evolving relationship has always been for your protection. When I was ready to shout the shit from the mountaintops, you told me you weren't ready, so I chilled. Now that I've respected your request, it's being held against me?"

"Imagine how I felt when I walked into Miranda's office today and saw a bouquet to match the color of her fucking hair? That's really some thoughtful, deep, gift giving. And you must have picked them out yourself because you certainly didn't have your house manager do it."

"You're unbelievable."

"Why did you buy her those flowers?" I ask again, demanding a better response than the non-answer I've been given.

He slams his hand on the table, and the dishes vibrate.

"To apologize for the shit I said about her in the hallway. My mother raised me better than that. Plus, I didn't want any animosity she may have been feeling towards me to blowback on you."

"How could that happen? I've already been hired."

"I don't know. I just wanted to to be sure. Like I said, she has family in high places."

"Have you told her about us?"

"No."

"Why not?"

"For the same reasons I have told no one else about us, to respect your wishes. You think that day in the vestibule felt good for me? We'd just made love the night before. We were holding hands because I was helping you inside the building, and the minute Miranda saw us you dropped my hand like I was on fire. I have fucking feelings too, Mia. This is not all about you. Your job, your bills, your knee, your fucking self esteem."

My eyes water. His words and the venom with which he's saying them are cutting me deep. When he realizes I'm on the verge of crying he panics and tries to backpedal.

"I'm sorry. Shit, I didn't mean that."

"You resent me. You resent everything about me."

"Not true."

"You just said it. I weigh you down like an anchor with all my shit."

"That's not what I meant at all, Mia. I'm just frustrated. I've done everything to take it slow with you, to not frighten you, but you're still running away from me and I don't want you to leave me."

I stand from the table.

"I think you and I both knew that this was a long shot."

"Don't you fucking bail on me, Mia."

"I'm just saying what we both knew was inevitable. We are better as friends, at least we were."

His eyes are wild with emotion.

"Sit down."

He walks toward me and slides his hand into my loose waves.

"You're talking reckless, Mia. We're better together."

"Let me ask you one more thing."

"Go ahead."

"Were you going to marry her? Is this big ass house and all the upgrades you've made over the last year to impress her?"

"Where are you getting this shit?" He begs. "I bought this house hoping that one day you and I would fill it up with kids."

"Tiger told me about you and Miranda. Evidently the entire team thought there might be a wedding."

The tears are too heavy to hold back, and they fall straight down the middle of my jaws.

"Baby, you know me. You'd know if I was getting married to someone. I would have told you."

"Were you thinking about marrying her? I mean, was it even a fleeting thought?"

"No. Never. I told you it was very casual between us."

I maneuver out of his grasp and look at him with a fresh new set of eyes.

Between us.

Just the reference sickens me.

"You're playing games."

"I'm playing games? You knew my feelings for you were changing way before you went out with Samuels, yet you did anyway, so who's the one really playing games with someone's heart? You're living with me, but you go on a date with my fucking teammate? Real nice."

"Yeah, but I wasn't *fucking* you then."

I make sure to throw back the word to him in the ugly way he said it to me this morning.

"FUCK!" he roars, and I gasp as all the dishes and some damn good lobster mac and cheese all go flying to the floor. He's out of control.

A bit of the cheese sauce lands on my cheek and I leisurely lick it off my face, grab my cane, and head for the steps.

"I'm not hungry," I tell him calmly. "And just so you know, the house manager doesn't do manual labor. Clean all this shit up yourself."

THIRTY-TWO

MIA

Do you remember how it felt when you got into an argument with your best friend in elementary school and now you're forced to dodge her everywhere you go. The swings. The water fountain. Gym class. It was a nightmare then, and nothing's changed now.

You would think on a huge training campus like this I wouldn't have to see Rush, but it doesn't matter, I feel him everywhere. We've eaten lunch, worked on therapies, done yoga moves and even had sex all over this facility.

The only reprieve I have is that we have no more one-on-one sessions together because he doesn't need any rehab right now. He works solely with the strength trainers most days outside of regular practice.

At lunch, I decide to eat at my desk and scour the web for a new apartment. It's obvious that the two of us are bringing out the worst in each other right now, and if I have any hopes of salvaging a friendship with him, I'm going to need to leave.

Although I'm not completely caught up on everything, at this point I should be able to afford something half-decent. I'm not looking for much, because one perk about this job is that I'll be on the road with the team during away games and staying in very nice hotels.

The one thing I don't look forward to is telling Rush about the move, though. He went through all this effort and expense to move me in, and now I'm leaving. He won't be happy about it my decision, but in the long run things will return to their natural order if I leave. He should be with a woman who has her shit together like Miranda, not the needy girl who's been clinging to him since college.

When I arrive back to the house after work, I notice there's a letter for me on the kitchen island that Rush has written. I'm not sure if he left it sometime this morning or if he returned home before me, but there it is. Short and sweet. Written in classic Rush Bacchetti chicken scratch.

Bird,

I packed a bag and am staying at the Marquis in New York City to give us some space. I know you're probably thinking about leaving the house, but don't. I don't want you to go. This is your home now too, and I need you to manage it. Don't bail on me now. And for your information, couples have arguments and so do friends. Everything is not always going to be a perfectly arranged love song.

-Rush

I spend the next hour sitting in the den and watching Peter, Paul and Mary swim around the fish tank and setting up my Instagram profile. It literally took me an hour to figure out how to add details to my profile and add my first post. I snap a picture of the sharks and post it. It feels kind of like mindless busy work, and I wonder how people do this on a daily basis.

I look at Tiger's profile and scroll down to check out some of his older posts. There are lots of pictures of him with players, a few celebrities and a lot of women including myself. I'm seeing that part of his "brand" is to post a picture with a different woman each time. None of the pictures look authentic. They all feel staged to align with his brand of being the most personable and popular player on the Nighthawks. At least that's how his publicist said he wants the public to perceive him. Safe and friendly means more endorsement dollars and a carefully crafted social media persona can help attract big money.

I like his most recent post and move onto another profile when my phone rings. It's Tiger.

"You're on the 'gram!"

"How did you know?"

"I can see who likes the posts in real time just like Facebook."

"Oh."

"Glad to see you're moving with the times."

"I still haven't figured out how to post a story though."

"Take a short video of your fish swimming and we'll post it."

"Okay."

I take the video of the sharks and Tiger walks me through how to post the story and add little stickers to it as well. I feel somewhat intelligent after I get it to work.

"I did it!"

"Now because you have no followers, no one will see it so what I can do is share one of your stories so my followers will see it. You're going to do the same thing you did except tag me in your story."

"Oh, boy."

"You can do it."

I create another story of the fish, tag Tiger's name, and post it again. Then he explains how he gets a notification that I've tagged him and then is asked if he wants to share it on his stories. It sounds very complicated and I don't totally understand but lo-and-behold I see Peter, Paul and Mary swimming on his stories and something about it is kind of cool.

"Thanks for the tutorial, Tiger."

"You have a killer aquarium by the way, Mia."

Ugh, and the lies continue.

"Thanks."

"What are you doing for the rest of the night?"

"I'm not really sure. Probably just watch a movie or something."

"You know they've got that whole watch party thing now on a lot of streaming channels. We could watch a movie together if you want."

"Umm–"

"I remember what you said, Mia. No mixing business and pleasure. This is just two friends watching a flick."

"Okay, any genres you prefer?"

"Action or mafia works for me."

"Action like a superhero movie?"

"Sure, I've seen them all though."

"Oh, I have too."

"I could watch Guardians of the Galaxy again."

"Not my type of eye candy, but it was a funny movie."

"Are you a Thor or Captain America girl?"

"Why just those two? I love them all."

Tiger laughs.

"Okay, we have to watch on our laptops. I'll send you the link."

I sit in the den with my last beer and a bowl of veggie chips and my laptop.

We're about twenty minutes into the movie when my phone rings.

It's Rush.

"Can we pause this, Tiger?"

"Sure."

"I've got to take a call."

"No problem, I'll go take a piss."

I mute the laptop just in case and pick up the phone.

"Hello?"

"So you're on Instagram now?"

I have the most incredibly bad luck.

"Yes."

"And you're taking videos of my fish and posting them on Tiger's Instagram?"

"That's not exactly how it works, but yes, and how do you even know that? I thought you didn't do social media."

"I'm trying to wrap my head around what would make you ever think that it was a good idea to post my fish to his gram? Like what planet are you living on, Mia?"

"Don't talk to me like that."

"Like you're over there losing your mind?"

"Like I'm some idiot, you always have to talk off the ledge, protect or save."

"Am I speaking Greek? Leave that fucker alone. I don't want you talking to him, doing social media with him, nothing with him."

"He and I are friends just like you and Miranda, I suppose. I saw you two yucking it up on the field once or twice. Same with me and Tiger. The difference is I have never slept with him."

"Mia," Tiger's voice comes out of my laptop speakers. "You don't have me on mute."

This night just gets worse and worse.

"One second," I whisper and actually mute Tiger the correct way this time.

I don't hear Rush on the phone any longer, but I don't think he has hung up either.

"Rush?"

"You're right, Mia. This shit isn't going to work. I'll give you by the end of the week to find another place to live. Maybe you can go stay with that motherfucker."

Then there's a click.

And deafening silence.

THIRTY-THREE

RUSH

WE'RE PREPARING for a preseason game to play one of our division rivals in Washington, D.C. The game is Sunday, so we have a few more days to prep. Physically, I am in the best shape that I think I've ever been. I have no injuries and I've bulked up twelve percent more muscle mass than last season. The point of training to become bigger and stronger is that it will be harder for a player to bring me down once I have the ball in my hand.

Mentally though, I'm a fucking wreck.

I am spending half of the time just trying to keep all the various plays in my head and the other half avoiding Mia and Samuels. It's hard, though.

Mia's leg has been bothering her more often lately, which always has me concerned, and sometimes I catch glimpses of her looking at me like I just shot a puppy in the head. Since when is she the victim? She's living in my house and doing who knows what the fuck with one of my teammates.

And don't get me started about his ass. He's strutting around here like the cat who swallowed the canary because they were on the computer together doing God knows what, and now he knows that Mia and I were seeing each other and he also knows that it the shit ain't good.

Yet with all of that going on, I've been the bigger person. I've been able to keep my distance and maintain some sort of calm reserve at work. I'm not going to lose my spot on the team and my livelihood because of what's going on with them.

I'm smarter than that.

At least I thought I was.

There's a group of offensive players in the weight room when Samuels walks in. My first instinct is to get up and leave after my last chest fly, but I don't want to give him the satisfaction. I've been kindly leaving the room or the area when he's come around.

Not anymore.

I didn't do shit.

"Mia worked me hard today," he says out loud, and I know the suggestive comment is for my benefit.

"Yeah, she's pretty tough. She's got my hamstrings nice and limber now," Carter agrees, oblivious to Samuel's real meaning.

He rubs his dick through his shorts.

"Mm, mine too."

His plan's worked because my body is now shaking with rage.

He's lying on the bench press and I swivel my feet around, grab hold of the dumbbell, and press it down to his chest.

"You say one more fucking word and I'll choke your ass right here and right now."

"Whoa, Rush!"

My teammates try to pull me off of Samuels, but I plant

my feet to the ground and hold my stance, pushing the dumbbell down even harder.

"Say one more fucking world and I'll rip your throat clean out."

"You should've told me," he squeaks out.

"I fucking told you."

"You should've told me she was yours."

"That wouldn't have meant shit to someone like you."

I lift the barbell because his face is turning a shade of beet red and the last thing I need is him losing consciousness. He dramatically holds his neck with both of his hands and takes deep breaths while the rest of the guys in the room just stare at me with slacked jaws.

"What did you tell her about Miranda?" I ask accusingly.

"The truth."

"What were you two doing last night?"

"None of your business. The way I heard it, she doesn't want your ass anymore."

This motherfucker.

I lean deep back and swing my fist straight for Samuel's eye and our brawl begins. Punches are thrown, barbels crash to the floor and we basically trash the gym. We keep throwing punches until Proctor and another lineman come in and help the other guys break it up.

"Rush, that's enough!" Proctor says for the room's benefit, but in my ear he whispers. "Good job, man."

Samuels definitely got the worst of it, but we both look pretty beat up. I go outside to the field to try and walk off my rage, but visions of Mia and Samuels doing freaky shit online, while she's in my house, keep playing like a loop in my mind. A part of me knows she never would do something so disrespectful, but the fact that I don't know for sure is what's killing me. Maybe this is what she was feeling about me and Miranda, but still... it's different.

I sit on the grass with my head in my hands for I don't know how long when I hear a golf cart pull up behind me. I lift my head, hoping it's Mia, but it's not.

"Hey, there."

"Hi, Miranda."

"You look a little worse for wear."

"Just a scuffle with some of the boys. It's good now."

"You sure?"

She sits down next to me.

"You know you can talk to me."

I raise my head and look at Miranda.

"When we were seeing each other, did you think we were serious?"

I can see my question takes her by surprise. But the only way to get it out there was to be direct.

"Well, yes, I did."

"Did I make you feel that way?"

"We saw each other every time you were home from being out of town. So, yeah, I thought we were dating. Are you saying we weren't?"

"I'm just trying to understand myself a little better these days, Miranda. It seems like I'm not to nice to strangers and I'm way too friendly with people I consider close to me. I've got to work on that."

"Oh, so this is about Mia."

"No, this conversation is about you and me."

"She's not right for you, Rush."

"No disrespect to you, but I don't think you're able to say anything about Mia. You don't know her, and if you and I are going to maintain any type of civil relationship, I need you to stay out of our business."

"I've been nothing but kind to her, but you two misrepresented your relationship to me."

"No, we didn't. We were platonic friends when I referred her for the job and things grew from there. But again, that's none of your business, Miranda. You and I are over and we've been over, right?"

"Right."

She stands and gets back into the golf cart.

"Get that face looked at, Rush. It's your money maker once you retire from the game."

"Will do."

As the cart drives away, I see Mia mid field. I don't know how long she was watching us, but I know it couldn't have looked good from that distance.

We both gaze at each other for what seems like an eternity, then she wipes what must be a tear from under her eye and using her crutches she limps away.

I hang my head in my hands and damn near cry myself.

Will I ever have my Bird back in my arms again?

THIRTY-FOUR

MIA

THE NIGHTHAWKS ARE PLAYING their fourth and final preseason game in New Orleans tomorrow afternoon, but tonight I'm sitting on the deck of my hotel suite in the French Quarter, stress eating two beignets and watching an old episode of *The Masked Singer* on my laptop. I'm waiting for them to unmask the snail I think, but honestly I could give two shits.

I'm learning that when the team goes on the road, it's our job to help with any ankle, knee or wrist wrapping before the game and to be on the sidelines in case of injury during the game. Otherwise, we aren't doing much.

I've always wanted to tour New Orleans, but I will not take a tour of a city by myself with this bum knee of mine. If I needed to run, I'd be up shit's creek. This would be a good time in my life to have a girlfriend to chat with, but sadly I don't have any. After my move to New Jersey, I gradually lost touch with my teammates and I only speak to Pearl on Christmas and my birthday. I was friendly with everyone I met at Phoenixville, including Mr. B, but I made no real friends there.

I didn't think I needed them.

I always had Rush.

It's when I'm most vulnerable like this that I make stupid decisions like call my mother and hope for once she could be a source of comfort to me. I know that's probably not a good bet to make, but I do it anyway.

Sometimes a girl just wants to talk to her mom.

"Mandy?"

"Mia?"

I can hear the confusion in her voice. This is actually very sad that her daughter calling her is a source of bewilderment for her.

"Hi, how are you?"

"Tired."

"Did you work a double today?"

"Well, no Mia, or I wouldn't be home."

"Right."

"So, what's up?"

"You got the check right?"

"Yes, everything's paid off for the year."

A thank you would be peachy, but I know I will not get it.

"Great, so uh, I'm calling because I need some advice."

"Advice?"

"Yes."

"Um, ok."

"I moved in with a friend to save money."

"Smart."

"And then me and that friend started seeing each other romantically."

"I didn't realize you were gay, Mia."

I sigh and pray that I can get through this conversation

with the woman who gave birth to me but clearly doesn't know diddly squat about me.

"I'm not gay, Mandy. I was living with a man."

"What man?"

"My friend from college–Rush."

Mandy is quiet for a moment. I'm not sure if she's trying to remember me even having a friend with that name or if she's angry that I moved in with a man and didn't tell her.

"So you're living with him?"

"I was."

"You were?"

"Yes."

"And where are you living now?"

"I have a room rental situation, but that's not what I want to discuss."

"Okay, what's the advice you need from me? I don't have a husband. I'm no expert on men."

"Well, like I said, things changed between us and I got scared. I mean, I wanted to trust that he was everything that he said he was, but then the whole Miranda thing happened and then the Tiger miscommunication and–"

Gah! I'm speaking gibberish. I'm sure Mandy can't even follow what I'm saying. It's like I started the story completely in the middle and she does not know how to follow along. This was a mistake.

"I don't know who a Miranda and a Tiger are, but I know for sure that the Rush boy has been waiting for you a long time."

"What did you say?"

"I said that poor boy has been waiting for you for a long time so you better not mess it up. He's a damn sight better than your father ever was to me."

"Why are you speaking as if you know Rush? You don't know him at all. I think you met him once."

I can hear her lighting a cigarette and taking the first pull.

"Oh, I know him. I got to know him the weekend you tore your ACL. He called me, damn near hysterical. Something about you going into surgery and being your good luck charm. I guess he felt guilty that he wasn't at your game that night, as if him being there could have changed anything. I told him plain as day that you weren't his responsibility, but he wouldn't listen. Guess that's why he got you that job."

"You know about my job?"

"What are you talking about, Mia? You've been working for that school since you graduated."

"No, Mandy, I was let go from that job. I work for the NFL now."

"Fancy," she comments as she takes a long drag of her cigarette. "How was I supposed to know that? You don't tell me anything."

"Let's back up for a second. What job are you talking about?"

"With the school, of course. Your friend pulled some strings with the president of that university and got you into that masters residency thing you were in."

"You're mistaken, my volleyball coach did that."

"I hope that's not what that lady-man coach of yours told you, because the Rush boy did all the string pulling. He's been sniffing behind your butt for the longest time. Glad to see that you've finally seen the light and gave him some. Just don't get pregnant. Then he'd probably dump you."

I can't breathe.

Tears stream down my face and plunk down on the ground like rain.

I sob so hard that I feel like I'm going to die.

"Mia?"

"I have to go Mandy."

"All right."

After I finish sobbing, I stare out into the beautiful streets of the French Quarter with mindless wonder as I retrace all my steps of my entire relationship with Rush. He's been there every step of the way for me, always playing the background, ready to catch me when I fell. How could I have ever doubted for one second that man loves me? Everything he's every done for me is the epitome of love.

I watch an elderly couple laughing and strolling arm in arm. Her hair is snow white and slicked back in a smooth bun, much like I wear my own hair, and he is bald and wearing a New Orleans cap that he obviously just purchased at a tourist shop. They are staring at each other like it's their wedding day. So happy. So in love.

I had that with Rush.

I know I did.

And now I realize I want it back.

I've just got some major groveling to do.

THIRTY-FIVE

MIA

**Regular Season
Nighthawks Vs. Eagles**

It's been five excruciating long weeks since our breakup and slowly Rush and I have found a rhythm at work that allows us to be at least... cordial. It's a tiny step in the right direction, but it's a long way from where I want us to be.

Together.

I find out during that time from Darius about some things that were said to ignite the infamous fight between Tiger and Rush that I heard so much about. Darius explained it was all over a woman although her name wasn't mentioned but that he was sure it wasn't Miranda. He also made a snide comment about Tiger deserving his broken nose, and when I asked him what he meant by that, he spilled the tea on Tiger and Proctor's mother.

"He's been on everyone's shit list for a long time. He was sleeping with Proctor's mom and not even being discreet about it."

My mouth practically hit the floor when he told me that. Clearly it was a key piece of information that Rush had kept from me, but only because he's a good man. He lives by a creed where he firmly believes that one shouldn't trash talk their teammates—especially if you can't actually verify the story. The whole time I thought Rush was being overprotective, and then being a jealous boyfriend, he was actually being careful and keeping me safe.

I decide I'm going to have to make a bold move if I'm going to get my man back, because we've already allowed too much time to pass in my opinion. Those are five precious weeks together that we can never get back, and time is a commodity when you're an NFL player who spends so much time preparing for games and then playing them.

I realize now that a lot of what happened is my fault (and maybe a tiny bit his). Everything is so extreme or so black and white with me because that's how I was raised. I've never lived in a space for grays because neither did Mandy. You were either a great father or a deadbeat. A liar or a truth teller. A dutiful daughter or a bad one. There was no in between, but I know better.

Things aren't always that simple.

And some things can never be explained.

Sometimes you just have to believe.

It's the first game of the regular season and we're playing my hometown team, Philadelphia, here in New York. The stadium is packed with season ticket holders and rowdy fans from both cities. The sky is clear, and it's a warm September day. It's glorious weather for the sport and an ideal time for me to make my statement.

I decide to ditch my normal PT uniform and wear a pair of fitted black joggers and an official Bacchetti 69 jersey to the game. Little does Rush know that today is going to be our coming out surprise party. Everyone is going to know (if they didn't already) that we belong to each other.

End of story.

Some players don't even pay attention when I enter the training room in my official Bacchetti gear, but the only person who matters does and when he sees me, he immediately freezes in place and his eyes lock on mine.

He's seated on a bench getting his wrist taped because of some continued tenderness after the fight with Tiger.

"Can we switch?" I ask Scott.

"Sure."

Rush watches me quietly and methodically wrap his wrist with the white bandage tape. When I'm finished, I raise my eyes to meet his.

"World domination greetings, Rush."

I anxiously wait for his response.

"World domination greetings, Mia."

"Ready to kick ass on that field today?"

"Affirmative."

We both smile and then I forward for a tight hug around his waist.

"Awwww," some players tease.

"Yo, are they fucking?" Another clueless player asks out loud.

"Don't get hurt and I'll see you after the game, Bacchetti," I tell him.

"After the game."

Out on the field, Rush is a monster. Even with a tender wrist, he sets a record for the most receiving yards in a regular game in Nighthawks history. It's understandably one of the most exciting games I've ever watched, although, I imagine I feel that way because someone I love is out their sacrificing his body play after play for the game.

Luckily the day went our way, and we won.

After the game there are some restorative therapies that we do for certain players who were hurt during the game, while the rest of the team are in meetings with the coaches. Then finally, after a long exhausting day, it's time for us all to go home and we'll start all over again in the morning.

I'm inputting some notes in my computer when Rush approaches me from behind with his large Nighthawks duffel full of gear and equipment on his back.

"You want a ride home, Mia?"

"I drove but thank you."

"You want to ride to my place then?" he asks.

"Sure, I'd like that."

***

I stand in front of Rush with nothing on but his jersey.

No panties.

No bra.

No ego.

This isn't what he brought me back to his house to do. He genuinely wanted to talk things through, because God knows there's a lot to discuss, but we have plenty of time for that later. Right now I need physical touch from him and I need it badly.

"I know we have a lot to talk about."

"We do," he agrees while sitting in the center of the modular couch in the den.

"But I've been thinking about this moment ever since I wrapped your hand before the game," I say.

I watch as his freshly showered dick grows hard right before my eyes in his basketball shorts, ready to have me at any minute.

"Rush," I breathe out his name. "I need you."

"It's been five weeks of pure hell for me, Bird."

"And me too."

"You can't just walk up in here and demand some dick like everything's okay 'cause it ain't."

He grabs his cock and strokes himself.

"I wouldn't dare to presume."

"Lift my jersey and spread your legs open for me."

I do as I'm told.

"Touch yourself," I tell her. "Touch your pussy for me."

I keep my eyes focused intently on Rush as I play between my folds.

"Slide one of your fingers inside your pussy."

I again do as I'm told, finding just the right spot and closing my eyes.

"Are you wet, Bird?"

"So wet." I tease.

He lifts his t-shirt over his head and I lick my lips as I watch the ripple of his muscles underneath all of his ink.

"Bird, come take my shorts off."

I walk forward, hooking my fingers into the waistband of his shorts and slide them down his legs. When his dick springs forth to life and angrily bobs up and down in front of me, I lick my lips again.

Rush places the beanbag chair on the floor in between his legs.

"Are you hungry for it, Mia?"

"Yes."

"Then bend down on the beanbag carefully and suck."

"Ok."

I pump my hand around the tip of his dick, and he groans into my touch.

"Now wrap that smartass little mouth of yours around it."

I open my mouth, sticking my tongue out to swipe at the tip of his dick.

He slides his hand in my hair and yanks my head up.

"I said suck on it, Mia, and don't stop until I tell you."

My eyes meet his, and I run my tongue from the base to the top of his enormous cock.

"Is that what you want?" I tease him.

He nods, unable to answer me with coherent words. The anticipation is killing him.

Finally, I stop playing games and wrap my lips around his dick. I savor it and take it slow, sucking all over him, like I want to taste every drop of him. As he hardens even more, I maintain my gaze on him as I pick up speed. I can tell that it's taking everything in him not to thrust as hard as he can in my mouth.

"Keep your mouth open, Mia" he growls out as he grabs the base of his dick and starts pumping himself.

I dig my nails dig into his thighs as he fucks my mouth.

"I'm going to come," he groans over and over as he floods my tongue with his release.

I swallow every drop as I wait patiently for him to tell me what to do next.

"Dammit, Bird, I think you liked that."

"I did."

"It was supposed to be a punishment."

"It wasn't," I say as I rub the ache between my legs.

He looks at me hungrily.

"Are you ready for me to fuck you, then?"

"Yes, please."

Rush scoops me up into his arms, and we climb the stairs.

"You're moving back in this week, is that understood?"

"Yes."

"And you'll get the surgery after the postseason, is that understood?"

I grin.

"Yep."

"Good, because my Bird needs to be able to dance at her own wedding."

"My wedding?"

"Yes, *our* wedding. Will you marry me, Mia?"

I think about the old couple from New Orleans and can so clearly see the two of us traveling and loving each other like that one day.

It's the dream.

The new dream.

"Yes, I will, because I love you Rush. I've always loved you. You are my best friend, my protector, and my lover, and I never want to leave your side again."

"I love you too, baby." He stops at the top of the stairs and gives me an emotional kiss. "You've always been mine to protect, as your friend and now as your future."

"Michael, play *Hopelessly Devoted To You* by Olivia Newton John."

Playing *Hopelessly Devoted To You* by Olivia Newton John.

"Let's go to our bedroom, Rush. Olivia and I are going to sing for you all night long."

Rush was the steamy hot baller who every girl would love to

have as a best friend, but **FREAK** is a sexy college phenom ready to make a deal of a lifetime with his tutor!

One-Click FREAK'S hilarious fake-dating, college football romance with a holiday twist!

(Keep reading to access bonus content!)

Thank you for reading Rush and Mia's story. As a special thank you for reading, I've written a **special extended bonus** epilogue. Grab it below.

GET THE BONUS INSTANTLY
https://BookHip.com/VWWNKCG

You can find all my extra bonuses here.
https://lisalangblakeney.com/private-ninja-room/

FREAK SNEAK PEEK

Please enjoy this sneak peek of the next book in the Nighthawks Series, Freak.

WEEK ONE

I literally feel like Carrie Bradshaw from Sex In The City (the actual show and not that questionable reboot), minus the beautiful designer clothes, and the fly-as-hell Upper West Side apartment.

Okay, actually the only similarity between me and that 1990s iconic fictional television character is that I've literally just been splashed with dirty street water by an Uber instead of a bus (like she was) and now my only decent-looking outfit is soaking wet.

"Ugh, you've got to be kidding me!"

It also doesn't help that when I enter The Links Cafe, the air conditioning is on full blast and my drenched dress clings to my skin, placing my nipples on high alert. Something told me I should have shoved a light jacket in my new Telfar tote when I was rushing out the door. I can almost hear my mother saying I told you so.

"Welcome to The Links Cafe." A slender woman with spiky salt and pepper colored hair and a white Links Cafe apron approaches me. "Would you like a table?"

"Hi, yes, but I'm meeting someone. There should be a guy about my age, thick blonde hair, and a tall athletic build waiting for me."

"Everyone in here is your age, honey," she chuckles. "Sounds like your guy is a hottie, though."

I have to laugh at myself as I look around the room. She's right. Cooper Grove University students occupy more than half of the tables in the eatery.

"Uh, yes, I guess you could say that."

Actually, he's totally hot. The man of my dreams.

"No offense to my patrons already in here, but I don't see anyone who fits the description you're looking for, but feel free to take a look."

"Is the air conditioning on extra high in here?" I ask, shivering in my damp dress.

"It's Georgia, hun'. The air is always on."

I eagerly scan the room, looking for the student I'm tutoring today. Aaron is a guy I've had a crush on ever since I stepped foot on the campus of Copper Grove University three years ago. Most students know and like him because he throws some of the most legendary parties at school, which is exactly why he doesn't know who I am. Why would he? I'm a quiet, nursing student who barely has time to eat, much less party if I'm going to graduate on time.

"I don't see him yet, so I'll just take a table for two, please."

"This way."

The woman grabs a couple of menus and seats me at a small corner booth.

"My name is Regina, but you can call me Miss Gina. Everyone does. Have you eaten here before, hun'?"

"No, ma'am."

"If you want a recommendation, I suggest the smothered pork chops today. They're the best thing on this week's menu. My husband is the chef, and it's his specialty."

"Oh, is this your restaurant?"

"It is ours," she says proudly. "We've been serving soul food to Copper Grove students for over twenty years."

"That's a long time. No wonder it's always packed in here. You're like a local treasure."

"Aww, thanks. We enjoy the community here as well."

Near the front window, I notice a fresh miniature Christmas tree with festive red and gold decorations that remind me of displays I grew up seeing in my neighborhood. I always get a bit homesick around this time of year.

"The Christmas decorations in here are gorgeous," I tell her.

"Aww, thank you. Christmas is my favorite holiday of the year. Can you believe that some of these decorations are from the seventies? They're basically family heirlooms."

"Like in the 1970s?" I ask incredulously. My mom saves nothing from last year, much less from decades ago, so I'm duly impressed. I still haven't gotten over her donating my beloved Barbie and Bratz doll collections to a local church without my consent.

"Believe it or not, we celebrated Christmas in the 70s," she chuckles, misunderstanding why I'm surprised. "In fact,

I would argue that it was much more fun back then. My mama didn't have to fight anyone in Walmart to make sure we had the toys we wanted."

I have to giggle. Miss Gina is funny. I like her already.

"I can't believe I've never eaten here before," I say, smiling, wondering how I could have missed out on a place owned by a woman who's obviously a CGU legend. I've noticed how everyone who walks inside the place greets her by name with a smile.

It saddens me that I've missed out on a lot of university traditions and fun because of my intense focus on my studies, but that's part of why I'm here today, doing something I normally wouldn't do. I guess in a way I'm trying to put myself out there and make up for lost time.

"Are you a freshman?" Miss Gina asks curiously.

"No, I'm a senior."

"A senior? I would have never guessed and, based on your accent, or lack of one, I can tell you're not from around here."

"No, I'm from up north."

"But you're staying in town over the holiday break?" Most seniors do.

"Yes, I'm here for the break."

I've stayed in Georgia every holiday break and most summers because I need the time to get my work done. I'm not necessarily the smartest person in the CGU nursing program, but I'm damn sure the hardest worker. So any chance I have to get ahead on upcoming courses that I know will be challenging for me, I do.

"Wow, a senior who's never eaten at The Links?" She smiles. "You're in for a treat, then. I'll send over your server once your hottie gets here."

"Thank you." I return her smile with one of my own.

I turn the camera app on my phone to check and see if I look how I feel, damp and gross. I try smoothing the fuzzy flyaways down of what used to be a slick ponytail when a massive human being almost gives me a baby heart attack when he slides into the booth next to me.

Not across from me.

But right next to me.

"Your hair looks great," is the first thing he says as he takes a seat.

What the hell?

As I inspect the huge stranger sitting next to me, I have to catch my breath for a moment because I've seen this guy before. I just don't remember where.

With a chiseled jaw and piercing hazel eyes, my stomach flips for a moment. But while he's ridiculously handsome, he also seems to have some major boundary issues.

Not cool.

I immediately scoot further inside of the booth to create some more distance and try talking reason to this inappropriate mound of muscle.

"I'm sorry, but you must have me mistaken for someone else. I think you have the wrong table."

He plasters a goofy grin across his face.

"Nah, I'm in the right seat."

I'm not sure if this is some sort of fraternity prank or what, but it feels as if all eyes in the restaurant are on us, which only makes me that much more uncomfortable. I don't like a lot of unwarranted attention.

"Can you at least sit over there, please?" I point to the opposite side of the table.

"Do you see me?" He gestures with his hands at the enormity of his body. "I can't fit in one of these damn wooden chairs. I need the room of a booth seat."

That's fair.

He's big as hell.

"Yeah, but do you have to sit next to me?"

"Where else am I going to sit?"

Now, I'm getting really annoyed.

"Are you playing games with me or something? We don't know each other. I'm waiting for someone, and you're in the way. This isn't a free table at the cafeteria. I'm paying for this seat, so move to another table. You can't eat with me."

"How do you know I go to CGU?" He wiggles an eyebrow and I notice a small permanent scar above it.

It's oddly sexy.

"What?"

"You mentioned the cafeteria."

"I just said that because I assumed. And why aren't you getting up yet?"

"Oh, I should have led with this when I sat down. The guy you're waiting for is not coming today, Willow."

My eyes widen.

"How do you know my name, creeper? And what do you mean he's not coming?"

My stomach drops.

I called in a huge favor with my professor at the student tutoring center to be assigned to Aaron during Christmas break, so now I'm wondering why he bailed. Did Aaron find out that I arranged this? If so, I won't be able to ever show my face again, because nothing stays secret on a small college campus like CGU. I'll be the laughingstock of my entire dorm. Gossip spreads through those five floors like wildfire.

"There was a switch at the tutoring center, and it's your lucky day. You're getting me as a student instead."

No, no, no!

It took me three years to build up the confidence to even figure out a way to meet Aaron. I mean, we've crossed paths a couple of times over the years, but our only verbal exchange was an awkward "excuse me" in the cafeteria line. I'm a quiet nursing student. He's a party legend. And never the two worlds shall meet.

This can't be happening.

"I didn't approve a switch."

"Professor Lee approved it. You can call him if you want to check," the behemoth assures me with a smirk.

"I don't have my professor's phone number on speed dial."

I wish I did though, because I don't believe anything that this overgrown kid is saying right now.

"Huh, you don't? That's odd because I do."

Is he being a smart ass or is he serious? I don't read subtext all that well. It's better when people are direct with me.

"Who are you?" I ask, slightly raising my voice, because I'm about ten seconds away from throwing these glass salt and pepper shakers on the table at this dude's head.

"You don't know who I am?" he replies with a dumbfounded expression, as if that's an impossibility.

"Uh, no, should I?"

"I'm Freak," he says in a self-important tone, as if that should explain everything.

"You mean you are a freak?" I sneer.

The colossal jerk raises a playful eyebrow as one side of

his mouth curves up and an enormous tongue licks the corner of it.

"I can be that too, darlin'."

One-Click FREAK'S hilarious fake-dating, college football romance with a holiday twist!

MIA'S PLAYLIST
(In no particular order)

Boom Boom Pow - Black Eyed Peas
How Deep Is Your Love - The Bee Gees
Bohemian Rhapsody - Queen
Man In The Mirror - Michael Jackson
Red Light Special - TLC
Shadow Dancing - Andy Gibb
Beautiful Day - U2
Would I Lie To You - Eurythmics
Hopelessly Devoted To You - Olivia Newton John

Spotify: https://geni.us/rush-spotify-playlist
Apple: https://geni.us/rush-apple-playlist
Amazon: https://geni.us/rush-amazon-playlist

YOGA INSPIRATION

THE NIGHTHAWKS

Have you read all of the books in the scorching hot
Nighthawk Series? Each novel features an alpha hot baller
and a happily ever after:)

Saint - Saint & Sabrina
Wolf - Cooper & Ursula
Diesel - Mason & Olivia
Jett - Jett & Adrienne
Rush - Rush & Mia
Freak - Freak & Willow
Brick - coming soon!

ALSO FROM LISA LANG BLAKENEY

The Masterson Series
Devour this addictive series about the possessive bad boy,
Roman Masterson, who falls hard and fast for the girl he's
promised his family to protect.
Masterson
Masterson Unleashed
Masterson In Love
Masterson Made
Joseph Loves Juliette
Masterson Box Set

Masterson Next Generation Series
The crazy hot fruit doesn't fall far from the tree. Dive into
this second generation of Masterson men!
Knox - Knox & Gigi
Bronx - Bronx & Karma
Seven - Coming soon!

The King Brothers Series
Dive into this series of interconnected standalones featuring

3 alpha hot brothers and the women they lay claim to
without apology.
Claimed - Camden & Jade
Indebted - Cutter & Sloan
Broken - Stone & Tiny
Promised - All King Brothers
King Brothers Box Set

The Nighthawk Series

Sexy & sweet sports romances set in the professional world
of football. All standalones.
Saint - Saint & Sabrina
Wolf - Cooper & Ursula
Diesel - Mason & Olivia
Jett - Jett & Adrienne
Rush - Rush & Mia
Freak - Freak & Willow
Brick - Brick & Kaya
Dak - Coming soon

The Club
(Also known as Bleu Whiskey)

Dark, age-gap, serialized romance set in the underbelly of
Los Angeles.
Patreon (early access)
Kindle Vella
Radish

WHERE YOU CAN FIND ME

MY VIP LIST (Get the nitty gritty)

I have a VIP Reader mailing list. I only send free books, new release, sales or special giveaway information to this group. No spam. You can join here:
http://LisaLangBlakeney.com/VIP

MY PRIVATE FAN GROUP (Casual fun)

Join my private Fan Group on Facebook also known as my "Romance Ninja Warriors" where I share all things new going on, celebrate birthdays, post teasers, yummy pics, giveaways and just chit chat.
http://LisaLangBlakeney.com/community

THE ARC TEAM (Book Reviewers)

If you are interested in joining my beta reader team then please join here: https://geni.us/N8jAU

ABOUT THE AUTHOR

Lisa Lang Blakeney is a USA Today Bestselling author of contemporary romance sold in more than 28 countries. Worried that her fellow PTO moms might disapprove, she wrote and published her steamy debut novel Masterson under a different title and pen name in August of 2015.

Thanks to strong reader support of her alpha male character, Roman Masterson, she was encouraged to continue with the series and published the entire Masterson Trilogy the following year. She hasn't looked back since and continues to write novels featuring strong alpha men and the smart women they seek to claim.

A romance junkie for sure, you can find Lisa watching a romantic comedy, reading a romance novel, or writing one of her own most days of the week. If she's not doing that, she's outside in the garden tending to her roses.

Lisa is the wife of one alpha (whom she met in college), mother to four girls, and two labradoodles. Get news on releases, sales and giveaways when you become one of Lisa's VIP readers at : http://LisaLangBlakeney.com/VIP

facebook.com/authorlisalangblakeney

twitter.com/LisaLangWrites

instagram.com/LisaLangBlakeney

amazon.com/author/lisalangblakeney

bookbub.com/authors/lisa-lang-blakeney

goodreads.com/Lisa_Lang_Blakeney

pinterest.com/lisalangwrites

tiktok.com/@lisalangblakeney

patreon.com/lisalangblakeney

www.ingramcontent.com/pod-product-compliance
Lightning Source LLC
Chambersburg PA
CBHW061539210726

48287CB00006B/2019